Club Medusa

Martin White

For my fellow writer, musician, ghost hunter and brother,
Steven James White
1968 – 2020

ACKNOWLEDGMENTS

Special thanks to the following fantastic and talented people for their help in helping me get this story out into the world: Kirsty White, Colin Brown, Matthias Bodner and James Ingham for eagle eyed editing, Amanda Nicoler and Swords and Scythes from Fiverr for top beta reading, Nik from Bookbeaver for the stunning cover, also to Andy McCaw and Deborah Chalmers for the lowdown on those two vital components for any good night out, alcohol and anaesthetics. Heartfelt thanks also to my amazing family, Kirsty, Logan and Lyra.

1. PROLOGUE

What do you really matter? Think about that.
There are almost eight billion people alive right now, how many of them do you really care about? What do you think the rest of them care about you? Be honest.

The fact is, most of us come and go from this life unknown. We live in clusters and layers dictated by chance, luck and money - and none of those layers matter to anyone looking down from the top. Even if you put yourself in harm's way to protect others, to make the world safer, you're still nothing more than fodder - expendable and consumable.

You can throw around all the first world, media friendly slogans you like, nothing will change the fact that we're all on our own here and the only things that might save you becoming part of the food chain are birth right and whatever club you might happen to belong to.
Sorry, does all this sound harsh? Nihilistic? Maybe it is, but I promise you it's true.

You probably think you're safe right now but trust me, you're never safe. What about all those people you just admitted you don't care about? The ones skirting around your life, looking at your money, watching everything you do online, listening to you through devices in your home, logging everything you buy at the supermarket? What

1

about the ones walking or driving past you on the street, drinking next to you in the pub, standing around the dancefloor in the club? You don't know them. Believe me, you have no idea what 'other people' are really capable of.

And if none of us really matter, that makes our world a very dangerous place…

2. PLAN

I used to believe blame was just a waste of time. It's a well-known fact that bad things happen to good people every day, so by the time you analyse any situation and work out where the buck should stop - you're too late, it's already happened - nothing is going to change that. I used to believe that, as long as you could *learn* from a bad thing, then all was not lost. All very liberal. I don't think like that now, the blame for *this* bad thing happening belongs to Gerry. Most of it, anyway.

As plans go, Gerry's had seemed simple and harmless enough. I would get the bus into central Edinburgh, we'd meet up, walk into the Old Town, visit a couple of old haunts, drink beer, reminisce, be careful not to mention the war, then go home – in that order. Probably the same as the plans of countless others that night - maybe with the exception of the war thing.

I'd known Gerry since way back, life always seemed to throw us together. We lived near each other when we were kids, went to school together, took a lot of the same knocks as teenagers, ended up joining the military together and eventually ended up serving in the same unit abroad -

seemed we couldn't get rid of each other. In short, we'd been down a lot of the same rough roads but somehow managed to stay mates through good and bad - especially the bad. The army had honourably discharged us both a couple of years before thanks to an operation in the Afghan going tits up and turning the pair of us into shrapnel magnets - but that's another story.

By then we were mostly used to the civilian life - we were older, arguably more sensible and pretty much getting the hang of what people did in the real world. We knew we had to be grownups now and with that came grown up problems. For example, the catalyst for our catch up that night was because he wanted to offload about a relationship breakup. Gerry had just been dumped by Melanie, the latest in a long line of girls who had probably seen his potential but couldn't quite manage to get him over either himself or his past. Not that I'm judging, it hadn't been so long since I'd found a relationship of my own where daily life seemed to actually work despite all the ghosts.

Also, because we spent so many years out the loop playing soldiers, Gerry and I both knew if we ever wanted to have 'normal lives', we'd better get a move on as we were already part of that 'late thirtysomething' generation, well past our crazy prime regardless of whatever shit we might shoot over a few beers. It was already a fact that during those last two years or so our number of nights out had dwindled. Now with my own new found stability I even had to check myself getting all judgmental when I ended up holding Gerry's jacket as he flounced off towards the ladies trying to cultivate some fantasy shagfest for himself. Something I would have to say, he rarely succeeded at.

Nevertheless, even if I admitted I was finally getting to that place I thought I wanted to be in life, I will take at least some of the hit for wanting to be there that night too. Well, I missed it all. I missed my mates, I missed the company. I missed the adventure, even if all it amounted to was wandering from place to place drinking, talking and trying to make each other laugh. Sometimes it just felt as if all the fun was slipping away from life as the years passed and we all got older. I may have been happy with my lot but I was already beginning to hear sounds of disapproval from my own partner about being 'out up the town.' Obviously I should have better, more mature things to do. So yes, maybe I did exaggerate the importance of giving my mate a shoulder to pretend to cry on. Maybe that does mean some of the blame belongs to me - but not much.

*

It was a Friday in late October and rain had been threatening all day. Even in the streetlight of the late evening there was still a sense that rainclouds were somewhere up there lurking, just waiting to drop their lot. Gerry had finished his shift at the hospital earlier that night where his job as a Porter served almost exclusively to pay the silly money gym fees he needed to keep himself muscle-laden and perma-tanned. I met him outside his Gym Club on London Road. I hadn't seen him in a while and he looked well. He was standing right outside the front door and clearly saw me on the approach.

"Hey mate, you still on the sex offender register then?" he asked loudly, which did the opposite of impressing two young girls who were walking into the club. I shrugged and looked resigned while he suddenly lunged forward and bear hugged me. All very manly.

"You're still an arse then?" I said.

"A taut and attractive one though," he replied smugly. I gave in and laughed. We did the whole insulting banter thing for a bit then ran through his plan again.

"That's fine by me," I said, "And launched by yet another fine woman too? How the Hell did you manage that?" He looked as if he was about to tell me - I cut him off, "No - no - don't tell me yet, we'll get a couple of beers in first, eh?" He shrugged and smiled, we probably both knew what had happened there. There was something else I had to ask him though, "Okay, let's get this over with early doors - how are you coping with, you know - the old stuff?" He knew what I meant and suddenly looked more focussed.

"I'm okay - still have my moments but I'm on a level. Not so much noise now - sleeping most nights, off most of the meds now. You?"

"Yeh, I'm good. I don't get much grief from any of it now. You'll get there."

We gave each other that look. Like most ex-forces guys we'd left our previous lives with some baggage that couldn't be dropped as easily as we (and everyone else) would have liked. Gerry had been especially unlucky, he'd had a really bad time with it - though I'd stuck around and helped him through the worst - as you do with your mates. We both shrugged.

"You remember the drill with the old stuff though?" "Please don't tell me you're going to make me say it out loud?'

I spoke quietly, "You know the rules, we don't speak about that stuff in public, even if it's hurting us bad. Too much drink, loud places, flapping ears, gung ho idiots and the way the world is right now, right?"

"Okay, I know. The Code," he sighed. I nodded, "Yeh, the Basil principle - don't mention the war,"

He shook his head, I stopped him before he went any further. I had to know he wasn't going to break down on me, "Any war," I added.

He shrugged non-committedly, I needed more than that.

"I'm serious, if you want to talk about that stuff I'm all ears and you know I'm here - but there's a time and a place and it's not out there among the drunken civvies. Are we good with that?"

"Uh. Okay. Sir." He paused and glared at me, then broke into a stupid grin.

"Screw you," I said. He laughed, we were good - and he'd taken the message. One more thing, "Oh, you got your mobile phone by the way?"

He looked at me as if I was sectionable.

"Are you serious?" he said, 'Why would I have one of those damn things on me?"

"Good," I said. It might have been a paranoid hangover from our past, but being visible from space to anyone who wanted to know where you were and what you were doing wasn't my idea of being off the grid for the night. Plus, they were annoying.

We quickly covered the short walk through the late evening pubbers in Greenside Place, up Princes Street and across the North Bridge. Before long we found ourselves at the junction with the High Street, The 'Royal Mile', outside our first nostalgia stop, the Bank Bar. It had an impressive sandstone façade and looked as if it may well have been a proper bank at some time, but to us it had always been a starting point, a place for the first and most sober talk of the evening. Also, it had a strategic advantage, as from there we could move off into whichever part of town we decided on without too much of a hike.

It was busy when we walked in; suits and smart casual all around, after work chat in the air. No one gave us a second glance as we ordered a couple of beers and found ourselves an empty table surrounded by chairs. We didn't exist to them, which might have been unfriendly - but it was fine by me.

And so to the formal declared business of the night. I listened dutifully over that first beer as he gave the story; a tragic, one-sided tale of how his latest relationship's last straw had come about. I made all the right noises as he described the melodrama step by step. As I remember, the script was similar to previous episodes where it had all been great at first but then the poor girl moved in with him and then Gerry's tendency to look after himself first became contentious. There were some faux comedy moments along the way where Melanie decided to restock his wardrobe with more 'age appropriate' clothing when he was at work and an incident where she'd given all his old vinyl away to a charity shop as it was 'getting dusty' - but overall, it didn't sound like the girl stood a chance. A dual ultimatum had been given where Gerry insisted she stop trying to change him or she would leave and she countered this by insisting he should 'grow up' or else she would leave. Or whatever.

Either way, the common factor seemed to be Melanie leaving, and leave she did. And also, as I'd suspected, Gerry didn't appear overly stressed or upset by it all. I was glad, I had to watch for that. In fact, life changing though this apparently may have been for him, I'm guessing he spent all of about fifteen minutes on the subject of the break-up - probably all of half his first pint. Was he putting a brave face on it? Of all people, I knew how to read him and I could tell he was probably more hurt than he'd admit. There were occasional pauses of uncertainty and sometimes he would let the words 'I suppose...' hang off the ends of his sentences - but he didn't seem like a man on the edge - or anywhere near one for my money. We both knew he just wasn't in the place yet where he could face the attachment and commitment, it was as simple as that. So ultimately, he got what he wanted - his freedom - but probably at the price of moving forward in life. At least, that was the way I saw it.

So there was no need to worry - he was stable. He was disappointed yes, but not a man in emotional freefall. In fact, as the time passed and the beers progressed, he made his thoughts pretty obvious that we should be finishing our evening off with post-midnight beer in a place where he might find some young, impressionable female company.

And that's where I came in. As I said, if there's any blame for the way that night turned out, it belongs to Gerry. I did not want to end up in any kind of late-night dancing den. I might have been complicit in going for a few drinks but my partner was already less than impressed with being neglected in favour of one of my manfriends on a Friday night, regardless of the circumstances. Plus I had work the next morning…

"Oh, come o*nnnnn*," Gerry drawled over the muted conversation and music, "This place is full of married women of *both* sexes - and it's way too bloody pretentious. Look at them - everybody's dressed the same with their craft beer and cocktails, sitting in their cliques swatchin' their phones - and that fucking jazz in the background is doing my nut in."

I couldn't disagree. We were sitting quietly at our table, but to the rest of the clientele we must have looked as if we had come from a different planet. Our leather jackets, jeans and Gerry's worn combats probably ensured from the start that if we were even noticed at all, we were going to stand out as potential carriers of the ned-plague by the chinos, Gap and Super-Dry set who, in our absence of many years, seemed to have moved in and made this place their own. I made hesitant noises but Gerry was relentless.

"The Clubs - that's where it's at now," he said, "'Juice' is on down in the Cowgate - 'Inferno' in Moray House - you know, even The Kitchen or The Attic down the road? Look Paul, you boring old bastard, I just want to get a bit dancing in, you know? Find a bit of a distraction for the night? Hey, look at me, I'm upset…"

He was a zoomer more like. That hadn't been part of the plan. I couldn't help but see what would happen if we went there; me falling home drunk and penniless at 4am, a dehydration headache and argument before leaving for work three hours later, then feeling and smelling like shit for the rest of the day with the prospect of even more grief when I got home. No thank you.

"Oh come *onnnn*, I just want to celebrate being a free man again. You don't even have to get involved, I can talk you up as my straight acting gay cousin so you don't lose any cred? Just tag along till we find some girls to talk to, then you can leave, honest!" There was now a whine of desperation in his voice, and I knew from experience that Gerry was notoriously stubborn with a few drinks inside him. It was beginning to look like there would probably be no escape. But who knows, maybe there was a part of me that still wanted to be able to play like that too?

"Not part of what I signed up for, mate," I said, realising my heart probably wasn't in the argument.

"Come on ya pussy, what's the worst thing that could happen?"

We had no idea. Stupidly, I relented - I deviated from the agreed plan.

"Well, okay. But this is for your benefit, understand? I'll be in a world of shit for being out after twelve and believe me I *will* be going home early enough so I can get a decent sleep before work,"

Gerry beamed triumphantly, he didn't give a shit.

"Hah! Good man!" he said, giving me way too heavy a slap on the shoulder which sent me lurching forward in my seat, "You won't regret it. And I'm telling you mate, I'm *telling* you, we're both too young to get written off yet!"

We finished our drinks and left the table. Our places were quickly snapped up by two well-dressed couples who had been hovering nearby. I hadn't noticed them at first but they'd appeared on my radar when I caught them indignantly glaring over at us a couple of times, presumably for taking up a table for four when there were only two of us. I saw the look of distaste, no, *disgust* on their faces as they skirted around to fill our seats.

"About time too…" I heard one of them spit out under their breath, I didn't catch which one. I was usually pretty intuitive with people and there was definitely a strong bad vibe from this lot, aimed solely at us. I checked back a couple of times as we moved off. For some reason they all held my gaze as if to say, 'Yeh, this stink eye is for you'. Their expressions told us we had a nerve taking up valuable seat space in *their* bar, Jesus, we weren't even dressed for it - what were we even thinking? I hated attitude like that, *they* were the young team around here, not us! I'm not one for feeling entitled but they clearly had no idea what Gerry and I had been through just to help keep their arses safe on those seats and their peaceful lives conveniently ticking over. I shook my head, broke off eye contact and trailed off behind Gerry towards the door. I threw them a final glance and saw they had all settled in to check their phones.

"So, is it just me?" I asked as we stepped back out to the High Street, "Or has everything really changed so much for the worse in this city?"

"Uh? How d'you mean?" Gerry replied, his thoughts elsewhere.

"I know it sounds like bitching, but it's just not the same, is it? No one wants to know you around here anymore. Did you see that lot that piled into our seats when we stood up? I see it every time I'm in town for a drink these days, it feels like everywhere is the same - every bar, every pub, they all seem to come with their own exclusive crowds. The whole city just seems to have a different feel to it now. I mean, please stop me if I sound like an old fart, but when we were the young guys doing the rounds, there weren't many places that would make you feel a total outsider like that. Even if nobody knew you there was always a bit of banter to be had, a bit of a way in." I was met by an indifferent silence.

"Please stop Paul, you sound like an old fart," he said. He didn't want to know. Once Gerry had some other destination in mind, half-drunken theories about social changes were going to be the last thing on his mind. I continued anyway - that hostile displacement in the Bank Bar had really gotten under my skin.

"Well, it pisses me off. It seems the only way to have a decent night out round here now is if you take your own clique of mates with you or study the frigging clientele so you can blend in with the wallpaper. You know, Google it beforehand, check the place out from the door, check the vibe to see if you're the right type of hipster to fit in?"

I looked round to see if Gerry was listening but his mind was already gone, dancing under the strobes with some lithe, young brunette somewhere.

He looked at his watch. "Okay, it's five past one now," he said. "The licencing curfew starts at half past, so that leaves us exactly twenty-five minutes to find a short enough queue to get into someplace decent before we get locked out for the night."

I shrugged, there was no point in pursuing it.

'Selfish bastard,' I thought.

"Lead on then," I said. Gerry gave me a sideways grin and without further discussion we both turned the corner and began the descending walk down Niddry Street, the steep crevasse of buildings which led to the lowest level in the old town: the Cowgate, our capital's night time party land.

3. DESCENT

Our destination was decided. Through recent years, the Cowgate had become the place to be if music, drink and no dress code were your thing. If you wanted to hang with the smartly turned out spending wads of cash you would probably head for the glitzy carnage of George Street and the New Town. If your thing was playing the shell suit lottery, you could fire on your finest casual sports gear and play the good bar/bad bar roulette of Lothian Road where the neds herded unpredictably. However, if you wanted occasionally decent music without too many contrived surroundings and fashion restrictions (but still with the overpriced beer), there was the younger network of venues which ran along the half mile or so between Bannerman's Bar in the Cowgate and the Salsa Bar in the Grassmarket.

But as soon as we walked a few yards down Niddry Street, we saw our first queue, a lengthy group of partygoers tailing up towards us from Whistler's Bar's front door.

"Nah," said Gerry immediately, as he eyed up the long line of bodies. "That's just a live music pub anyway, not hardcore enough,"

We squinted through the windows as we walked past and saw it was jam packed. I liked the place, I'd seen some good local bands there but tonight it was shoulder to shoulder - so I concurred. We walked further down Niddry Street until we had to step off the pavement on to the cobblestones because of the crowds outside the other bars. Finally, Gerry started to converse.

"Anyway Paul, you seem to be forgetting something about us these days,"

"Like what?"

"Like, when you were on about things not being the way they used to be?"

"So you *were* listening?"

"Yeh, 'course I was. But it's *never* going to be the same again, is it? We're both getting on a bit you know, even a bit wrinkly if I might be so bold. We started drinking round here about, when - seventeen, eighteen years ago? Longer maybe? We're just tired old gits now to all these kids and students."

"Thirtysomethings if you don't mind,"

"Yeh maybe, but I mean, when we were younger, everybody else was too - guys our age just weren't on our radar. In our day we had our way with the ladies and it felt like everybody was our mate. Nowadays if we step into any of these places we probably just look like dads on the pull."

"It doesn't stop you trying to hump their legs though, does it?"

"Ha! Well?" he laughed, "I reckon I've got a responsibility there, you know. Every young girl needs a tale of heartbreak where some uncaring guy sweeps her off her feet, promises her the world then turns out to be an arsehole, leaving her in tatters. The way I see it, I don't mind being that awful bloke their new boyfriends are going to have to be better than. I'm providing a service by setting the bar so low."

I gave him a dismayed look and saw that 'I've-had-a-few-beers-and-no-one's-going-to-stop-me' grin.

"You're a twat," I said.

"Yeah, whatever, Mr Loverman," he drawled, "So where do you think we *should* be going then?" he asked, "A Bromide bar, maybe? Church? The 'Jurassic'? That'll get your droop on for sure…"

"I don't know," I said, "And also don't care. But don't count on me hanging around till closing time, this guy here is not up for an all-nighter."

Gerry said nothing more. As we walked further down the centre of the steep, cobbled road I glanced at him again and found I knew the look on his face well. It was the grin of Gerry's alter ego, the evil twin who was going to have his way no matter what. We both knew that after all, if we failed everywhere else we would still have a chance of blagging our way into the place we all knew as Jurassic Park, the old ballroom in Tollcross, a Club that unashamedly catered for the more 'mature' end of the nightlife market. Jesus, that was almost us…

A few seconds later we reached the bottom of Niddry Street where the imposing stone buildings of the Cowgate rose up to their highest all around us. It was common knowledge, at least to anyone who had been on a guided tour around there, that two or three hundred years ago, to save space and keep the city from growing beyond the City Wall, the town planners (for want of a better term) did most of their new building either on top of any houses that could take the weight or any other existing foundations around at the time. Upwards instead of outwards, that was their vision. It was also common knowledge that because of all that constricted building in the Old Town there were still scores of known and unknown passages and recesses everywhere. Further up the High Street there were still entire unaltered streets of buildings preserved underground. Some had just become uninhabitable, obsolete and obscured over the years while others were sealed off and ruthlessly forgotten around the time of the plague, tragically left alone only to be turned into horror themed tourist traps since the millennium.

But down in The Cowgate this was level one, year zero (well, maybe 1400-ish) - and the streets didn't run any lower than that. This part of the city rose up in layers of thick-walled, vaulted stone warehouses accessed by open passages from the street, passages us locals have always called 'Closes'. Even among the crowds and the bright lights at night it always seemed to me that the deeper you ventured down here, the more of the past you saw in the buildings, as if that walk down Niddry Street to The Cowgate really was like some sort of architectural time travel.

However, the Cowgate these days was anything but forgotten. As we turned right at the foot of the Street, we saw the bustling stretch of nightlife before us. From then on, we were constantly sidestepping and giving way to others, passing as we did, bar after club only to see queues of revellers outside that seemed to go on forever. There was no problem finding somewhere to drink down here - the problem at that time of night was getting past the licensing curfew imposed by the Council, the by-law that declared at 1:30am prompt, there was to be no more admission to any pubs or clubs, regardless of their closing time. No amount of pleading, bribing the doormen or whining on Facebook would get you past the gatekeepers for that all important last hour or so and tonight it seemed as if everywhere was teeming with expectant hopefuls in queues, constantly checking their phones and watches. We walked the whole length of the bustling street and ended up being no further forward. Gerry looked at his own watch and scowled.

"Fuck," he said. "Five minutes left to get in somewhere," I stayed silent but my urge to escape was growing. I was already at my time limit and I knew if I could ride out these last few minutes I still stood a chance of making it home in time for at least some sleep and minimal earache from Gerry.

Our route took us past the last cluster of drinking dens on the south of the street then under the dark archway of George IV Bridge. We stopped on the pavement at the off-street walkway which led in to Shady Lady's Bar.

"Hey, there's not much of a queue outside Shady's," said Gerry, excitedly.

"I'm not surprised," I said, "It's a dive and usually full of daft wee laddies wanting to prove something," This was a place I'd never been fond of. I'd had a bad experience there, admittedly it had been years ago but that once was enough. It was the usual story, I was in with friends and we just weren't part of the crowd, which that night seemed to be scrawny, gangster wannabes. From what I remember, I'd been unintentionally served ahead of some of them at the bar at one point and caught a few of them giving me the 'hard stares' afterwards because of it. Or something. Later on, there followed a typical cliched, cock measuring contest - I left my own company to go to the bathroom which gave some of them a chance to follow me out to the stairway. I was then given the whole 'who the fuck are you shithead?' routine from the smallest, mouthiest one - basically the prelude to being attacked. I knew I had to be proactive as there were too many of them, so without engaging, I picked out the biggest one, lunged without warning and put him down hard, scattering the rest in the process. I stepped back and readied myself - but the rest had been taken by surprise and backed off slowly, now unsure what they were dealing with. Don't get me wrong, that's no war story and I'm no action hero hardass but I didn't see any other option, I had to do something they would understand. As it happened, it did the trick - as far as they were concerned I was now seen as being 'more mental' than they were and therefore no longer considered 'game'.

It blew the night though, I had to move everyone out when I got back as I knew it would only take another beer or two for resentment to kick in and a reinforced crew was despatched to take another shot. It's shit when some idiots ruin your night like that. So yes, Shady's may well have changed since then but as far as I was concerned, a Club lives or dies on its first impressions and that place was not my idea of a good time.

"Come *onnnn*. It's a place to go. It's beer and music, man," said Gerry as he began to stride off the main road towards the end of the short queue. I paused and thought about complaining - but then walked wearily after him, hoping I'd never see the inside.

As we joined the line, I checked my watch. It was a couple of minutes before half past one and there were still at least half a dozen bodies ahead of us. 'We still might not make it,' I thought hopefully. But even then, my stomach was in a knot. For some reason I had a very bad feeling in my gut about being there, something I couldn't quite explain; a discomfort that felt like it ran deeper than just the fear of hangovers and falling out with the neds inside.

Just before that magic minute was upon us, the doors opened to release a deluge of noise, light and drunken partygoers. They laughed, shouted and sang out of tune, dancing obliviously past us towards the main road and the chance of a taxi. Their night was probably over now - lucky them. Two men by the doors caught my eye. A couple of stewards wearing black flying jackets with "Lady's Niteclub" embroidered on the front began to wave the people directly in front of us into the club. By this time a few more bodies had drifted into the line behind us, obviously as hard up for a beer as we were.

My watch now said 01:32; I said nothing.

Another minute or so passed before the larger of the two doormen, a hulk of a guy physically blocking the doorway with his frame, looked at his watch and silently nodded to the other; a small, wiry looking guy with lank, fine hair and a drooping moustache which may or may not have not been ironic. He seemed to be in charge as he had the clicker in his hand for counting people in and out. His face was set in a scowl and his whole demeanour screamed 'Wee Man/Big Chip on Shoulder: avoid.'

"Okay, folks!" barked Wee Man. "It's past that time and there's no one else getting in here now! Move off home please!" I heard mutters of discontent behind us and turned to walk off back to the Cowgate along with the rest of the unsuccessfuls, working out how best to disguise my relief that our wild night out had harmlessly come to an end.

"Well, I guess that's it," I said to Gerry as I turned, "Come on, I reckon that rain will be on soon anyway…" But it was his pissed off alter-ego that replied.

"What? No fucking way! They can't do that to us!" he hissed, slowly shaking his head. I sighed, this was not a good sign. Gerry, for all he was a good mate, also had previous for being a liability with a few drinks in him and whilst he was never one to start any trouble, as long as his evil twin was around he'd never walk away from any either. I tried my best to sound diplomatic, "They just did. Look, you know the way it works with these guys," I said, "They've got a little bit of power here and they'll make a big deal about using it - now back off."

"No way!" Gerry argued, "I counted eight people coming out there a minute ago - those bastards only let six in."

"Gerry, leave it, there's no point, remember the kind of guys you're dealing with here…" But there was no stopping him,

"Don't worry, I'll be polite," he said. That usually meant trouble.

"Hey, you two!" he was shouting at the doormen now, "There were eight bodies came out of there a minute ago, you only let six in - that's hardly fair guys!"

"Sorry, mate," hissed the smaller doorman, "We're just doin' a job here. Now do us a favour and piss off somewhere else." With that he stepped forward into brighter light and I got a better look at him. Again, I was getting that whole 'wee man/nervous aggression' vibe off him which was probably helping to stoke the bad feeling in my gut. I also saw he had a name-badge on his jacket just under the club logo, his name was Norman. Norman the doorman, Jesus, give me a break.

4. CONFRONTATION

But Gerry wasn't about to see the amusing side.

"That is fucking ridiculous," he continued, "Even you plums must be able to count to eight? They had to come out in single file to get past us, I watched you count them out on the clicker!" Norman shrugged, put his clicker in his pocket and said nothing - but I saw a smile grow slowly under his moustache; he was enjoying the confrontation.

"Or maybe it's just 'cos we just don't like the look of you two whingin' arseholes," the bigger one laughed. He also stepped into the light and I saw his name-badge simply said 'Al'. I didn't need to overthink things to see this was a flashpoint situation. Where I tended to ignore most doormen if they started the 'el cheapo hard man' routine, I knew that right now Gerry would only see it as a blistering red rag to a bull.

"Or, maybe it's because you're just a couple of fucking *dickheads* who can't count the number of fingers on one hand!" ranted Gerry. Okay, shots fired on both sides now but still manageable. This wasn't like the drama I'd had in the club before, I just needed to get him out of there. I stepped over to Gerry and put my arm around him in a

21

'come on, you old drunken mate, you' sort of way and started to guide him off.

"Leave it Gerry, this won't get us anywhere." I said. He quickly shrugged me off. I saw Norman was bristling at this exchange and had now turned around to speak into a hand held radio. I also saw his larger colleague clearly fumbling for something under his jacket the way someone might reach for a weapon. Surely that was just for show?

Gerry continued his 'reasoning', oblivious to what was going on around him. "So - what do you say? You let us in and we'll all be friends or I take your incompetence up with the management?"

"I know," snarled Al, "Why don't you just go away and fuck yourself in the empty head?" I could tell this was sending Gerry ballistic. That was enough. I moved forward again and reached out to grab Gerry by the arm; flight was clearly the safest option for everyone here. But Gerry stepped forward before I could grab him and mouthed off some more.

"What the fuck d'you think...?"

But he stopped dead as Al suddenly pulled out a short, black baton from the fold of his jacket. He slapped it down hard in his hand for effect and walked menacingly towards Gerry. Behind him Norman still cradled his radio, his voice now rising in pitch, demanding that whoever was there should 'Send the boys down to hand these tossers their arses.' As always, it was surprising how little time it took a bad thing to grow from absolutely nothing.

With hindsight of course, this was the point where both of us should have abandoned all self-esteem and just ran. I still remember standing there weighing up the possible outcomes like a kid watching a fight about to kick off in the playground. Comparing Gerry to Big Al, if it came down to size alone it might look like a fair match, but what this muscle-bound sentry wouldn't know was that unlike a lot of other weight grunters, Gerry backed up his bulk with aerobic exercise, mostly by way of hitting things: MMA, boxing at least and if you asked him, the list would probably go on - and send you to sleep. It was one of his coping mechanisms. My guts were still leaden with the overpowering sense of risk, not of losing any fight but of winning it - and then having to explain to the suits afterwards how stupid and puerile it had all been. I turned and tried to make a show of walking away, hoping Gerry would just snap out of it.

"Come on mate, you know these guys aren't worth it, get your arse over here now!" I shouted with a bit of tone, hoping it might spark off some of the old discipline in him and praying he'd snap out of it before we both came to blows between ourselves. But no, he was now fixated.

"And who the *fuck* do you think you're going to scare with that thing?" Gerry mocked, standing his ground whilst Al, like a prize twat, maintained a threateningly slow approach towards him, probably waiting to see if he'd bottle it and run.

And so it began, those next few moments that changed our lives forever felt like an eternity, yet were over in a flash - but I suppose that's the way it is with most fights.

Without a further word spoken, Big Al accelerated as he closed in on Gerry, raising his baton in a high, kinetic arc over his last couple of paces. I watched the baton swing down towards Gerry's face - but he smoothly drew his hands out of his pockets, threw one arm up and easily blocked the blow. Barely a heartbeat passed before a counter punch was delivered straight to the doorman's face. As contact was made I heard the crunch of cartilage and saw an almost instant flow of blood from his nose.

This sudden violence grabbed Norman's attention. He turned from his radio to look over at the three of us. Now that physical blows had been traded he was clearly out of his depth, his face an expression of stark horror. Al reeled from the blow. He threw his free hand up to his face then pulled it away almost immediately looking strangely surprised to see the mess of red, wet matter in his palm. He looked at Gerry with a glare that said, 'I'm going to kill you for that,' and growled. Al then lunged at him with all his considerable weight, but was neatly sidestepped by Gerry, who saw him coming a mile off. As Al passed him harmlessly by, Gerry spun with him dropping his hand down firmly to the back of Al's shaven head, guiding him skilfully downwards as he passed through the empty space where - a fraction of a second before - Gerry had stood. Al was now in a critical position, off balance and lumbering. As I knew he would, Gerry moved in to end the confrontation with minimal effort as his leg hooked out Al's stumbling feet, sending him off balance and tumbling straight towards the ground where he landed with an ungracious thud.

Gerry stood where he was, shaking his head, looking at the sprawled doorman - probably thinking of some Hollywood style one liner to finish the moment - when I checked his back and saw Norman had suddenly sprung into action. He was fast, I hadn't expected that and I was surprised he'd found the bottle to get involved - but then as he moved, I saw a flash of metal in his hand glinting in the streetlight. In that split second, I realised he had pulled a knife and it was about to be buried in Gerry's back. I don't even remember shouting a warning as I launched past a bewildered Gerry and grabbed a hold of the knife-wielding arm of Norman.

Thankfully he wasn't particularly solid and I managed to stop him short before he found his mark. He yelped as I squeezed his wrist hard, trying to twist the blade around and out of his grip. He was stronger and wirier than I'd expected too and straight away he started thrashing himself around taking me with him. Despite his size I felt as if I properly had my hands full. I yelled at him to drop the blade, probably more for the benefit of anyone who might have been watching (or worse, filming) and missed the fact that this was a defensive move on my part. But now he was too far gone, despite my best efforts he caught me with his other hand and planted me square on the face. Bastard. Straight away I felt blood run in my own nose and down the back of my throat. I shook my head to clear the shock - there was no way I was letting go of this guy now.

"Fuck's sake!" I heard Gerry gasp behind me as he caught up with events. Next thing I knew, Gerry skipped forward and planted a side kick in his stomach, knocking the breath and the fight right out of him. As he doubled up I held on tight to his arm then gave it a hard twist which caused him to keel over and drop the blade on the ground, where it bounced and clattered away behind us along the walkway.

With Norman also down, Gerry and I exchanged looks of disbelief. This couldn't really be happening to us, could it? I wiped the blood away from my upper lip. My nose was throbbing, but I'd had worse.

Then, in what must have been the very next second, I saw Gerry's eyes draw to a point behind me. I anticipated what was coming next and ducked as Gerry lunged past me towards where Big Al had fallen. I whipped round to see Gerry fully launch himself at Al, who had obviously recovered from his takedown quicker than expected and was on his feet, the discarded knife now held tight in both hands - he'd clearly lost the plot and now meant to do some real harm. Gerry swept his arms heavily to the side and grabbed him - in a heartbeat their bodies became tightly locked together, each struggling viciously, a tangle of limbs with the occasional flash of dangerous metal in the mix.

I quickly stepped over and tried to intervene, to free the knife for a second time. I gripped one of Al's arms with all my strength, but he hauled away using his weight as a lever and threw me off balance. Still with my hands locked around his arm, he spun and all of us toppled down towards the ground. As I pushed my arms out to break my fall, Al viciously snatched his own arm back into the rolling struggle. Then as the heavy mass of bone and body rolled over on the cobblestones, there was a stark, tearing sound followed by a prolonged murmur and the watery hiss of escaping breath. I froze - I knew that sound. As I looked on I saw a pool of thick, dark liquid begin to spread out from underneath the tangled bodies.

For a few seconds both bodies lay deathly still. Then, as if some kind of sudden realisation had struck him, Gerry pushed himself up quickly to reveal the wooden handle of the knife protruding from out of Al's chest. There was an obvious line of blood streaked right across the front of Gerry's shirt.

Despite all our training, everything we'd lived through and learned in combat - a moment of panic sparked between us.

"No. No way…" gasped Gerry, "What the fuck are we going to do now?"

My own mind was also racing.

At that moment, the twin doors of the nightclub were thrown open and five burly figures emerged from out of the light and noise beyond. All were dressed in the same black flying jackets as the first two and all appeared just as big as Al, their silhouettes blocking out any view beyond the doorframe.

Gerry turned his head towards the approaching group and I saw his fists clench - he was going to go for it. I gripped his arm hard - this time I got his attention.

"I think we're going to run," I said

5. RUN

We set off at a sprint making our way back towards the Cowgate, knowing the countless dark passageways and closes there would be the best place to shake them off. As we reached the main street we began dodging and weaving around taxis and drunken bodies, spurred on by the rising threats and screams of our pursuers, who hadn't wasted any time in giving chase. From what I could hear there was no point in either of us running as we were both dead men already. Faces and cars flashed by as startled pedestrians swore and pissed off car drivers blasted their horns in our wake. We stopped at nothing, sprinting as fast as we could, trying to keep a decent amount of space between us and the mob.

By the time we reached the close that separated the converted church-come-nightclub, Wilkie House and the Kitchen Bar next door, we'd managed to put a fair bit of distance between them and us. I was just thankful those meathead types usually ran out of breath pretty quickly.

Gerry and I scrambled around the corner almost losing our footing at the speed we took the turn. Inside narrow, dimly lit close we straightened ourselves up and slowed to a fast walk. We both knew this was a good call as this passage led further into the bowels of the Old Town and there was more than one way out - it gave us options.

"Should we split up?" Gerry asked on an exhale.

"Too dangerous," I breathed, "They're really pissed off. If they caught either of us on our own we'd never stand a chance." He knew I was right.

"Better lose them then," he said, but at that I heard the threatening screams grow nearer as if they were approaching the entrance to the Close. I'd hoped we might have slipped their line of vision in the crowd as we made the turn, but then I didn't want to stop to judge the distance. Both of us bolted onwards up the inclined path and steep stairway which led past La Club Angele, until we took a further turn and emerged at the top of the climb amongst the high tenement flats of Guthrie Street. Again, we slowed to match the speed of the walking crowd. This street was pretty much student residential, lined with newish university flats built after a gas explosion levelled half the original street years before. Student flats on a Friday night meant lots of late-night activity so there were more bodies there making it easier to mingle and blend.

"Where to now?" Gerry asked, the bastard was hardly even out of breath. I found myself wishing I'd kept my fitness up the same way he had. I glanced around - we could have run south into Chambers Street but that was a wide-open road blocked along one side by the Museum - no place to hide if we were spotted. We could have tried one of the other closes and hid till later but that just wouldn't be tolerable - far too high a risk of them getting lucky.

"Back down," I gasped.

"What?"

"Back down to the Cowgate - under the arches at the Court building and up the next close on the left,"

"We just came that way!"

"Just do it..." I barked, there was no time for persuasion now, he had to be ordered.

Gerry said nothing more and followed on. If I was right, the mob would follow us through the Close we'd just left, then assume we would keep moving further away once we reached the far end. My plan would take us back on ourselves but if we ran downwards in Guthrie Street we would emerge on the Cowgate further back from where we'd turned off. We set off at a run and a glance behind told me we would be around the corner, out of sight before any of the mob reached the top of the steps behind us - they wouldn't know for sure which way we'd gone.

Within seconds we were back down in the busy Cowgate, jogging along the stretch of pavement towards the cover of the foundation pillars under the towering Court buildings above. Now it was only the occasional homebound partygoer giving us any sort of passing looks, so we slowed and stopped beside a row of piss-soaked waste bins there. I chanced another look behind us - nothing obvious I could see. We were now standing at the foot of another narrow, high sided close which led away from the Cowgate into the cover of a parallel side-street beyond. We began a brisk walk up the passageway doing our best to avoid the fresh pooling of urine on the steps. As we neared the top I saw the black and gold street sign fixed on the wall high above the summit: 'Dyer's Close,' it said - how appropriate.

At the top of the steps we stilled ourselves as best we could to listen for any sound of pursuit. There was still a drunken cacophony from the far end of the close mixed with distant screams which may or may not have been the masses still enjoying the good times beyond. We lingered a few seconds and listened to drifting voices exaggerated by the echo off the high stone walls - but the screams became more and more indistinct. If the plan worked, our pursuers would have assumed we'd taken the obvious escape route from Guthrie Street to elsewhere in town and with a bit of luck they would now be searching in the wine and jazz bars of the Southside. With a bit *more* luck, they may just have made a few wrong turnings themselves and ended up completely lost - it was easy done. For the first time I found myself quietly thanking those bygone town planners for the infuriating layout of this part of the city.

We were now in the next street up, a cul-de-sac with one end blanked by the imposing entrance to the Sheriff Court, the other leading to a narrow one-way street between Greyfriars Churchyard and the Cowgatehead below. The street felt oppressive, dominated and darkened by a massive low stone archway, the underside of a road bridge above which spanned one side of the street to the other. It was effectively a dark stone canopy which, at its lowest parts, had just enough headroom to allow pedestrians to clear it whilst walking underneath.

Conscious of the CCTV cameras peering our way from the court entrance, we walked away from them as casually as we could to a point around half way under the arch where we stopped to catch our breath. Fit or less fit, both our chests were heaving with the unexpected effort and shock of it all - but it seemed for that moment at least, we were safe.

"Christ..." I gasped. I found it hard to put my racing thoughts into words.

"I..." Gerry gasped, the exertion finally catching up with him, "...didn't mean to..." he was still looking numb. He shook his head, "*Jesus* - it wasn't my *fault*..."

But it really was - and he knew it.

"That guy looked as if you'd finished him back there," I said. Gerry responded by looking morose and clasping his hands behind his head, pulling it down to stare at the pavement.

"You know what we should do?" I spluttered. I wasn't entirely sure if I knew myself or if I was asking Gerry.

There was a pause punctuated by our breathing and the sound of my own heart pounding in my ears. Then, as he often did, Gerry offered a late reply,

"Yes. Yes, I know what we should do - be sensible. Go to the police and tell them what really happened - go through all that 'our side of the story' crap." Even after all this he could still manage enough sarcasm to make me want to kick that 'bad fuckin' attitude' all the way out of him. I somehow got the impression that despite everything he still wasn't prepared to redeem himself like an adult. I felt my temper fraying further,

"*Yes!*" I was shouting now, "Bloody right, we *will* go to the police - and we *will* tell them what happened down to the last detail! There's no way I'm going to be running away like some criminal because some macho fuckwit doesn't know when to go home!"

Gerry shook his head slowly but kept his eyes fixed straight down. He knew I meant what I said and he knew I was right. We both also knew it would never be that simple.

"So we explain it to the cops - then, as soon as word gets through their intel systems the spooks from our old job will find out - and then we'll have to try and explain this whole sorry clusterfuck to them," I looked over at Gerry whose head bowed even lower at the thought.

I turned and slammed my fist hard into the wall. Frustration, anger, fear - everything was now fogging my head, wooling my thoughts, stopping me from thinking clearly. I was also picturing the wall being Gerry's head at that moment - but we were past fighting among ourselves, that would only draw even more unwanted attention. Just like the old days - in the worst possible way - we still had to work as a team. The pain in my staved hand helped as a throbbing reminder not to start losing it.

I began to pace the cobblestones while Gerry continued staring downward, trance-like. I worked on getting my thoughts into some kind of order as my breathing and heartbeat reduced. I became aware of the night air feeling cool through my shirt and jacket. I took some deep breaths - keep the head - be logical you twat.

"Alright," I said eventually, "Alright. Okay, it *was* an accident. You might have been behaving like a fucking *two year old*!" I felt the anger rise again as the words came out - I raised my hands - no, calm down, start again.

"...but it *was* unintentional," I said, "It really was. The big guy came at you with a blade, I saw it happen. He looked as if he'd lost the plot, as if he was really going to use it - you were using *necessary force*." The phrase from the past stung us both. Gerry slid to his haunches and cupped his hands around his face. He gave out a deep sigh from behind them.

"Jesus!" I took another deep breath and looked up at the brick underside of the archway above, pacing a few steps out on to the road. How the hell were we going to get out of this one?

But when my gaze returned to street level, my heart missed a beat. Two girls had been watching us from the pavement at the edge of the bridge, obviously listening to everything.

6. HAVEN

They were standing silently in the shadow of the arch maybe fifteen feet or so away, smoking cigarettes and leaning casually against the iron street railings outside the tenements. The stone canopy deadened all the sound under it and I knew our voices must have carried. Had they been there all along? Probably. Shit.

"You boys in some kind of trouble?" asked the smaller of the two. I lifted my hand up to filter out the glare of the streetlight behind them and saw she was a slender girl with pale skin and dark blonde hair that hung around her shoulders. Her silhouette outlined a slight but defined figure in what looked like some sort of dark one-piece catsuit. Not so practical for the shopping I thought, but her poise was so casual and confident that somehow it looked just right. Anyway, who was I kidding, dressing like that would barely even register around the Old Town clubs on a Friday night.

So - what to say when lost for words. Blurting out the whole sorry story would be stupid but God, it would have felt good to offload to someone, to unburden some of that blame and vindicate myself, even if just a little. The conflict must have lit me up like a beacon as I stammered to say something that wouldn't sound like a lie.

"No." I said. It sounded like "Yes."

Both girls turned to one another and whispered, the second girl bending forward slightly to hear what the blonde girl was saying such was their difference in height. It seemed as if there was some sort of hurried debate going on. I didn't like it - I felt as if I'd been put on hold while they conferred.

Then as my eyes adjusted to the backlight I began to see more detail. The blonde girl was young - they were both young - probably early to mid-twenties, but there the likeness ended. The other girl was taller, just short of my own height with a mane of long, black hair which parted in the centre and from a severe fringe, flowed evenly down the sides of her face and back over her shoulders. She looked lean and was dressed more plainly in what looked like a man's white shirt and worn, black leather trousers. Her arms folded in front of her as the conferring continued, the tip of her cigarette glowing, held at just the right angle to let the smoke drift away from her clothes. There was no denying both these girls were attractive – but they also looked as if they could handle themselves in a fight.

I suddenly became aware I was paying them far more attention than I should be. Daft wee lassies - maybe some other time. I paced back over to the crumpled form of Gerry, still with his head in his hands. I kicked him gently as a prompt to pull him out of his fit of woe. When I looked back up, I saw both girls scrutinising him. After a second or two, both glanced at each other and nodded almost imperceptibly, a movement so subtle I surely would have missed it had I not been so strung out. The smaller one spoke again,

"Do either of you happen to have mobile telephones I wonder?"

Seemed an odd question, "Funny you should ask – but no." I said. A glance and a slight nod passed between the girls as if that was just what they wanted to hear.

"It's just, well - you wouldn't get any reception under that bridge," she added.

Bit of a puzzling introduction I thought.

"Okay. Where did you two spring from, anyway?" I asked, trying conspicuously to hold my voice steady.

Gerry looked up to see who I was speaking to. As I suspected he might, he quickly rubbed his face and began to push himself back up in an effort to regain some credibility in light of the sudden female company.

"Hmm." said the dark-haired girl, "We just came up for some air - it's just a wee bit stuffy down in the Club."

"What Club?" I asked, dreading the answer might be Lady's.

"Medusa." she replied quietly, and nodded over her shoulder down past the railings. I assumed there were probably some recessed steps behind her leading to a door below street level. That wasn't unusual, a lot of bars and shops in the Old Town were accessed the same way - but I couldn't recall ever having seen one here before. I stepped forward to take a look and as I moved closer I realised there was muffled music coming from somewhere below and behind them - something was obviously going on down there after all. I heard Gerry shuffle up behind me.

"I've never heard of that one," he croaked.

"No, you won't have, we don't advertise," said dark-haired girl.

I turned and looked at Gerry - this was wasting time, we needed to be away from here and fast. He shot me a look that asked 'what are we going to do now?'

"Well, it looks like you're in trouble to me," said the smaller girl with a gentle barb of insistence. She nodded towards Gerry's bloodstained shirt which I realised looked very obvious close up. Gerry folded his arms as if it would

35

immediately make the mess disappear and began to stammer something which was cut short.

"Oh, you're hurt too," the taller girl directed at me. In a swift movement which took me by surprise, she quickly stepped forward and wiped some of the blood spatter off my shirt with a handkerchief she must have had balled in her non-smoking fist. In the earlier chase I'd forgotten all about my burst nose.

"Err... thank you," I croaked. She smiled, clutched the handkerchief then stepped nimbly backwards to her friend, quickly folding her arms again.

"I'm Keisha," said the blonde girl. "This is my best friend, Teagan."

"We do *everything* together," said Teagan with a mischievous smile. She knew it was a cockteasing cliché and I wondered if she meant it as a joke. Keisha took a final draw on her cigarette and threw it down on the pavement, stubbing it out with a small Doc Marten boot.

"Maybe you'd both like to come down and join the party?" she asked.

"What about the curfew?" asked Gerry.

"We don't have a curfew, it's a private party, no licence, nothing to do with the Council or anyone else here," said Teagan, "Don't worry though, we have all our permissions, it's all legal, we just run it as a sort of - co-operative." I turned to Gerry and nodded silently. Yes, it was a plan - a place to go to get us out of sight meantime. He quickly nodded, understood.

But the exchange was broken by the sound of shouting behind us,

"*Look*! That's them there! Pair of *baastaards*!" I turned to see two of our earlier pursuers emerging from the top of the stairway at Dyer's Close. In a heartbeat they quickened their pace and made towards us. I saw both had weapons in their hands not unlike Al's baton from earlier.

"Come *ahead* - you *FUUUUUCKS!*" the biggest one screamed with as much venom as he could find. He broke into a lumbering run and I saw in his face he was intent on nothing but hurt. Both girls seemed strangely unfazed by this - but we were going to have to do something, and fast.

"Okay, maybe you two would be *safer* if you came downstairs with us," said Keisha, with a disturbing air of calm.

"I think so," I said quickly. At this, both girls turned and nimbly fled down a steep set of steps which led from the pavement to a sturdy looking door in the tenement just below street level. Gerry and I hastily followed and watched as Keisha gave a series of knocks on the door, obviously coded. Bizarre. As seconds passed I noticed there was a white mask hung on the wall adjacent to the door, a sort of masquerade face with messy, red lines striped across the eyes. Maybe it was the clubland equivalent of putting balloons up outside a house where the party was. My heart began to pound as I heard the footfall of approaching thugs echoing in the archway above.

But within the space of a few heartbeats, the door swung open and we were quickly ushered inside. I was the last to step through the door and as I did so it swung heavily shut. Metal scraped on metal as a large iron bar slid coarsely across its back, locking it down. Our pursuers must have been right behind us - but where I expected to hear banging on the door as soon as it was closed, I heard nothing. Maybe they were keeping 'eyes on' and calling reinforcements? Yes, probably that.

Once inside I saw we were in a reception room of sorts. The lighting was strange here - ultraviolet strips hung suspended overhead with strings of cheap looking fairy lights pinned around the walls – there was enough light to see but it was still gloomy and odd. Immediately behind the door there was an old cloakroom desk which had obviously seen better times, a few old looking wooden chairs, some out of date notice boards lay at odd angles around the walls and on the main wall above the desk, a crisply unfolded map of the world with a number of pins stuck in it, seemingly at random. Ahead of us there were twin doors with oval windows pulsating with light from beyond - probably the main part of the club. In all, it looked to me as if we were standing in some old, disused disco bar that had hastily been put back into service.

"Don't worry," said Teagan to Gerry.

"You'll be safe with us," said Keisha to me.

"Just wait a minute." A man stepped out of the shadows behind the doorway, this must have been the guy who closed the door. "Who said you two could come in here?" he was looking directly at us, his eyes a malevolent stare. This doorman was different to the usual crew, he wasn't particularly big or tall but the neat cut of his black suit and dead looking eyes gave him a sense of subtle menace. This was no bone headed thug; this man had an air of being truly dangerous.

Keisha spoke for us, "It's okay Vincent, we've asked them in as special guests." Teagan then drew up close to his ear and pursed her lips as she quietly whispered the words, "*Cochon longues...*" Some kind of password? I wasn't sure if I was supposed to have heard it or not - maybe it went along with the coded knocks. The doorman nodded slowly, tolerantly, his steely expression didn't falter and his eyes never left mine.

"Just don't cause any trouble," he said to us slowly, "We don't tolerate trouble from outsiders here." Normally this would have had my back right up, but all Gerry and I could do was nod compliantly - it was clear this guy didn't negotiate and with the wrecking crew undoubtedly gathering outside, these people were now holding all our cards. I was the one to break his stare by looking over at the bolted door. If anything, at least it looked more capable of keeping the lynch mob out for the moment.

"Come on guys," said Keisha, as she walked off. We turned and followed as they led us over to the double doors where we could see the coloured lights flashing through the glass. Above them I saw a sign crudely painted above the doors glowing neon green in the ultra violet, it said: "Club Medusa - Enjoy."

I knew it was wrong, but I couldn't help but admire the backlit figures of both girls as they slinked through the doors and turned to hold them open for us. An old Grandmaster Flash track was playing inside, the bass rumble took me right back to my younger days, probably the last time I'd heard it. Strangely, Gerry and I both paused there as if something were holding us back. I glanced round and saw he was giving me a look. I could read him – something wasn't sitting right here. I knew, because I felt it too.

"Gentlemen please?" said Teagan, gesturing us to enter. But we knew we were committed, the only way to go now was forward. We walked through the doors into the music and took in the view.

The layout of the sprawling cavern inside wasn't unusual for this part of the Old Town - it was a low room made up from a series of interconnecting stone vaulted chambers and alcoves. The central part of the club with the dancefloor was easily seen from the entrance doors but beyond that the room was broken into sections divided by stone pillars which formed a series of open archways surrounding the middle of the club. Although it looked as if the place was probably a good size, very little could be seen from any one viewpoint without peering around pillars or walking into alcoves. Low lit passages led off from the main part of the room in all directions while stone recesses seemed all around, asymmetrical and darkened. It was gothic alright, but then virtually every other pub, club and shop at this level of the city was much the same, most choosing to make the vaulted cellar look a feature rather than spending a fortune renovating.

In the centre of the room was a large and new looking, probably temporary wooden dance floor with a few bodies dancing on it to the thump of the bass. On our right was a crudely lit mobile disco where the huddled figure of a DJ fidgeted in the lamplight with an arrangement of decks and mixers. Teagan broke off from us and immediately made a beeline for him.

At the farthest side of the dance floor was a well-lit table on which lay the remains of a large buffet, leftover food scattering its surface like scraps left at the end of a hungry wedding. Arranged randomly around the room were seats of all different types and sizes; some looked as if they were built into the walls but there were also odd-looking sofas and wooden chairs arranged around a motley collection of tables. Nothing matched, it all looked begged, stolen or borrowed.

And as if that wasn't enough, the patrons appeared every bit as odd and varied as their surroundings. It was difficult to make out the fine detail through the disco strobes but there seemed to be almost every size, shape, age and gender imaginable in the place. From nimble looking pensioners to middle aged, conservatively dressed parent types, goths to young trendies, academic sorts and young girls like Keisha and Teagan - it was oddly surreal. As I scanned around further, I couldn't help but notice that regardless of all this diversity, everyone appeared to be mingling, seemingly engaged in cheerful conversation.

Gerry nudged me, "This place is beginning to ring a bell," he said, "I'm sure I ended up in here at the end of a session a couple of years ago, not long after - you know, the thing we don't mention. I was pretty gashed - don't remember much - just that this was some late-night pub no one ever came to unless everywhere else was closed."

"What was it like back then? I don't suppose you remember the ways in and out?" I asked.

"Looked pretty much the same as this from what I remember, a bit of a dive. I don't remember coming in the way we did, but as I said, I was pretty well out of it. I think the entrance might have been a bit further down the main road. Place wasn't open for long, went bankrupt I think. Looks like somebody got hold of the licence and opened it back up - at no expense obviously…"

My eyes were drawn to a group of four or five Latino girls on the dance floor, obviously trying to speak to each other over the strains of the music. Then, almost as if we were the point of discussion, they turned to us, smiled and waved - as if they knew us. I waved back awkwardly then swiftly turned away, feeling my face burn as if I'd been caught looking.

I began to do what I should have been doing - scanning for potential escape routes. Nothing seemed very obvious. There was a bar to our left - it seemed a spartan affair with a few makeshift optic stands and mismatched mirrors propped up against the wall like afterthoughts. Below the line of their reflections were wine bottles arranged in rows along the back wall. Strangely there was no one standing there propping up the bar and no obvious bar staff waiting to serve either. Then my attention was drawn back to the outline of Teagan as she weaved back towards us across the dance floor.

"And if you ever decide to stop gawping and get us some drinks, we'll have two medium bodied chardonnays, please," said Keisha, which made me realise I'd been staring again. I turned around to see Gerry was already halfway across the dancefloor heading in the direction of the bar.

"Sure, of course - two medium bodied, err - chardonnays," I said.

"We're just going to the bathroom," said Teagan, and both walked off towards the dancefloor then in towards a

41

recess on the left, chatting as they went. This time I couldn't hear a thing either of them were saying over the music. I joined Gerry at the bar. When I got there, I shot another quick glance back at the girls and saw Teagan holding something up to her nose and mouth. For just a fraction of a second, she turned and glanced over at me - then quickly turned away. I could have sworn she was nuzzling that bloodied handkerchief from earlier. No, that would be gross - probably just itching her nose. Get real.

7. PARANOID

The bar seemed minimal. I scanned the line of optics, most of which were crudely nailed to a wooden plinth above the bar and saw there wasn't much choice. A bottle or two of Chartreuse, an almost empty bottle of Absinthe, some Ports and Sherries were all there but the usual suspects such as whiskey, vodka, rums and gins were all noticeably absent. I couldn't see any beer taps so I guessed they must have sold it bottled. They did have wine though – some bottles were uncorked and lined up against the back of the bar, I could see more still in segmented cardboard boxes stacked against the rear wall. From the pale greens and clear glass of the bottles I guessed whites were popular. Just as well.

"They want white wines," I said to Gerry, who was already holding a £20 note up in full view to attract the attention of the absent bar staff. He nodded and lowered the money, we were obviously going to have to wait.

"Well, what do you think?" he said, as he turned and looked around.

"I think they'll still be outside and we're still screwed,"

"No, about this place?"

I turned again and took in the scene. It still seemed odd, this mismatch and merging of furniture and generations - as if it really was some sort of hurriedly organised gathering of a strange family.

"I don't like it," I said, "All a bit weird for me. I mean, I'm bloody glad we got in here when we did, but something about this place isn't quite sitting right."

"Oh, come on ya naysayer," said Gerry, obviously wanting to believe.

I shrugged, there was no point in dressing things up to make him feel better. "Look mate, we're in a tight spot as it is, the last thing we need right now is any more grief. It all seems a bit convenient for me, those girls had no reason to invite us in did they?"

"Yeh they did - they saw we were in the shit so they did the right thing!"

"Maybe. Or maybe it was them who got lucky? They saw we were in the shit and all out of options? For all we know this could be some kind of honey trap setting us up for a massive taxing when we try to leave. You know about all those scams in the Soho clubs, right?"

He nodded, "Jesus Paul, yes I know about them - I'm just trying to be positive here. Look, you saw the cut of the door on this place and you must have got the vibe from that guy working it? I doubt he'll let anyone in they don't want. And all these people, they seem, well – they seem normal, there are grandmothers here for fuck's sake! I'm getting a weird vibe too but there's no way this is some London bait club and so far I'm not picking up on any threats. I think we'll be safe enough here for a while, at least until things cool down outside, right?"

I relaxed a notch, Gerry seemed calmer now and he was actually speaking my own thoughts out loud. I knew that leaving would mean either a straight surrender to police or fighting through the mob outside - and at that moment I didn't fancy our chances with either. We really didn't have much of a choice.

"Okay. For the record, I'm not convinced by this place - but we'll stay here for now and see what happens," I scanned the dance-floor again, "At least the folk seem friendly enough,"

Then Gerry raised his finger as if something had just occurred to him, "Hang on," he said, "Can you see anyone with a mobile phone in here?"

He had a point, "Now you mention it - no I don't…"

"Ahh, *bonjour* gentlemen!" a voice purred at us from behind the bar. We both turned and saw a barman had materialised just as suddenly as the two girls had earlier. He was a heavy-set, middle aged man with cropped hair dressed in a black Tuxedo. He smiled widely and peered at us through thick-rimmed glasses, his hands clasped expectantly in front of him. He was awaiting our orders.

"Uh, can I have two - err - medium bodied chardonnays please," I said, "And two beers."

"Beers?" the Barman looked quizzical through an unfaltering smile.

"Yes, some bottled lager please? You know, Millers, Stella, Bud - something like that?"

"Ah, umm...yes. It's just that - we don't have a terribly large amount of *beer* in stock, sir. Tell me, are you invited guests?" The barman's accent was an uncomfortable mix of BBC English and a hint of west coast brogue - it sounded put on. I struggled to think of the best way to explain our presence in the Club. "Er, yes. Keisha and, um..."

"Teagan," said Gerry.

"They met us outside when we were walking by and - err - they asked us to come in."

"Ah right, I see." said the Barman, "If you'll excuse me one moment I'll just have a wee look down the stairs and see what we've got." The barman lurched off around the corner of the bar and ducked down through a low, narrow door which I presumed led to the cellar.

"A bar with no beer," said Gerry, "This could be a threat right enough,"

I used the break to scan around again, I didn't like the way there only seemed to be one way in or out of this place. As I did so, the bass thump died down and the music took a bizarre left turn as 'Would?', an old Alice in Chains track began to play. Jeez, I loved that song. It seemed an odd choice for the company here tonight but I wasn't complaining. More bodies both young and old moved onto the dance floor and began to sway to the hypnotic riff.

"Sorry, gents I do apologise," the well-spoken Barman returned behind us, "We're all out of beer and such this evening, I'm afraid we only have a few spirits and porters left, as well as our special selections of wine of course. We do only tend to provide drinks which directly complement the food."

Gerry turned to me in dismay, mouthing the words 'No beer? Help me…'

"Fine, we'll have two of the same then," I said. "Let's not complicate things."

"Ah, an excellent choice, sir." the barman glowed, "The acidity in the Chardonnay complements the food exquisitely! Let's see, the house Chardonnay at the moment is a particularly pleasant, err…" he turned around and lifted a bottle from a collection at the back of the bar, glancing at the label as he did so, "…this one," he beamed. This guy clearly had no idea, he was winging it. With that, he began to empty the contents of the bottle into four glasses. He flamboyantly threw the empty bottle spinning into a large, plastic rubbish bin near the cellar door and placed the glasses in front of us. Gerry handed him the twenty.

"Oh, no no no!" said the barman, sweeping the money away. "Did my young friends not explain the monetary arrangements?"

"Sorry? Is it all on tab or something?" Or could I be right about the bait club scam?

"Oh no sir, this is a private party tonight, all refreshments are provided and are complimentary for guests - it's one of our traditions. The Club is a co-operative you see, run by subscription so we don't have to worry about bar and food prices on the night,"

"So there's food too?" asked Gerry.

"Yes, of course!" the barman continued with grin so seamless and sincere, it only made me more nervous. "If you've just joined us then I'm afraid you've missed the first course, but I'm sure you'll be fully included throughout the rest of the evening,"

Gerry looked to me and smiled, "See, it's fine - like the girls said, it's a private function - these folks have just hired the place out for a party. I think we've actually landed on our feet here, mate..."

That explanation fitted of course, and it did seem to make sense. Hell, maybe I was just being paranoid.

Then something caught my eye - I glanced over to the double doorway, the main entry to the Club, a sudden movement through the windows in those doors – but then it was gone. I stilled myself and watched - and there it was again, frantic movement and then it passed, something moving fast beyond the doors in the ultraviolet. Then, a sudden flash of what could have been an angry face flashed by one of the windows. I was too far away to see any detail but could that have been one of the doormen from earlier? I nudged Gerry and nodded towards the doors so we had two pairs of eyes on whatever was happening. However, as soon as Gerry caught on, more and more bodies seemed to suddenly want to get up and dance mid song, obscuring our view to just the occasional glance. From what I could see now all I was getting was the impression of moving silhouettes. Then, after a few seconds, the window cleared, all movement stopped - and no one came through the doors.

I spoke quietly, "Did you see any of that? Looked like some sort of scuffle outside. If we're staying here we should make ourselves discreet," He nodded quietly, understood. He picked up two wine glasses and followed on as I skirted around the outside of the dance floor, making my way to a seating alcove I had spotted opposite the entrance. From there we had a clear view of the only confirmed way in - but it was far enough away to give us a heads up if any trouble came through them. We sat down at a wooden table surrounded by five wooden chairs which probably would have looked less out of place in a grandparent's hallway than a back-street nightclub. My chair creaked and complained as I rested my weight on its frame. We put down our drinks and sat in silence for a minute or so listening to the music and watching those doors to see if any trouble might come through them.

Eventually Gerry spoke, "Okay Paul, I've been thinking 'bout all this," I moved forward to hear what he was saying. My chair groaned accordingly, "You're right, we should go to the police."

I nodded quietly.

"It's the only way - I mean, it *was* an accident and it *was* one of them who pulled the blade. That was way out of order in anyone's books even if I was giving them a hard time. You can vouch for that, I mean, it was self-defence, right?"

I nodded, "We'll still get a rough ride though, and that's just with the civvy police."

"Yeh, but we don't want to make things look even worse by running away. Well, any more than we have done already. Look, I'll happily take the hit for arguing with them as long as you tell the cops about seeing them pulling the knife."

"Gerry, all we need to tell them is the truth. Those guys on the doors are supposed to be professionals, pulling a blade on some bellend just for insulting them is way off the scale."

Gerry nodded, he rolled with the insult graciously but neither of us felt much like bantering. We were both hunched forward at the table now. I found I still couldn't take my eyes off the doors where I'd seen the commotion earlier.

"Okay - there's something else," said Gerry, "But I'd be breaking the principle by telling you, so if you don't want to hear it, say now,"

I knew only too well what he meant by 'the principle', our mutual agreement not to mention anything in our previous military lives. We'd masked it by calling it 'the Basil principle' after an old episode of Fawlty Towers where 'don't mention the war' had become a catch line. But since 9/11 everything had changed, there were ears everywhere and it would only need one idiot and a social media account to drop us deeply in the shit - so, to us it was no joke. I looked around, no one was in hearing range, the music was most likely too loud for anyone else to hear us as long as we were quiet. It was a risk though, it was always a risk. I made the call.

"It's been a clusterfuck tonight so I'm guessing you've got a good reason. Make it quick, keep it quiet - and if you start losing it on me we shut it down, understood?"

Gerry nodded, I knew he understood and I knew that *he* knew the principle was for our own good. Like anyone else with our type of past we both had some dark baggage - and as soon as we discharged, the little support we'd been given had just stopped - after that we were on our own. It felt harsh, especially after the dark shit we'd done for our country - but it was what it was and if the forces teach you anything it's to shut the fuck up and get on with it. He leaned in a little closer and spoke a little more quietly.

"That last tour we were on, you know, none of the false flag stuff we got dragged into before?"

I nodded again, at least he didn't want to talk about stuff that could get us murdered just for mentioning it.

"That evac outside Deshu," I felt my own back tingling, all those memories were hurt, but especially that one. It had never left me either but I nodded him on, he needed to get something out.

"I know we've talked it to death and - it's not *usually* as big a thing for me now," His brow furrowed, he looked as if he was choosing his words carefully.

"You know, we got those girls out of the compound, we got them through that desert in the dark - we were almost at the RV - then we realised we had an extra girl there?"

I nodded, going over it was taking me back there too, I knew what was coming but needed to know what his point was.

"When that kid knew her cover was blown and she pulled out that grenade - the sound of the rest of the girls screaming when they knew they were going to die. Do you remember I couldn't get that sound out of my head - like - at all?"

I nodded nervously and quickly scanned around for anyone who might be taking an interest. No one I could see.

"Yeh, I know, that was your biggest thing - worse than the shrapnel."

"Right - but, with the Docs and the meds and you - and a lot of time - it got better. I had most of it pretty much shut out by the end of last year."

I still wasn't sure where he was going with this.

"Right,"

"Well, I'm more than happy to be in this place and I know I argued the case for staying earlier - but ever since we came in, just after we stepped in those front doors, I swear I started to hear those screams again. It's like - they're still in the back of my head - but starting to push their way out to the front…"

I raised my hand, he'd said enough - not just about our past but about the Club too. I remembered the moment we'd had in the reception area - almost like a shared bad vibe. I knew that other than the place being a bit odd, Gerry was right - the doorman aside, none of the crowd in there looked a threat, but I knew if it was affecting him like that, especially after what happened earlier we'd have to get out of there sometime soon.

"Okay," I said, "I get it and I'm with you mate, we can't stay here long,"

He nodded, we both understood. "Paul, don't worry," he said, "I'm on top of it - I'm pushing them all back down where they should be – but they're still there…"

We sat in silence a few seconds more, then he took a deep breath, as if returning back to his usual self.

"So, how long do we wait till we make our excuses?" he asked.

I ran the options in my head – what was our best strategy? I looked at my watch - it said 02:10hrs. "This place won't be open forever, I reckon we wait till three, it'll probably close about then like everywhere else and the streets will be busiest. By that time, the bonehead will have been carted off to hospital,"

"Or the morgue," Gerry added. I ignored his remark even though he was probably right,

"And by then the police will be guaranteed to be looking for us. They're bound to have spoken to Norman, that twat who pulled the knife in the first place."

"Yeh, like he's going to tell them what really happened,"

"Right, so the police will want us bad - so we'll go straight to them. I reckon when we leave here we walk straight back down to Lady's along the main roads - no closes or dark passageways. That place will be crawling with cops now. We'll get a hard time - especially if Norman's got his version in first - but at least if we're with them we should be safe from the lynch mob."

"Okay, what if the cops come in here looking for us?"

I sat back in my chair and shrugged, "We tell them the truth: we were chased in here and were too scared to come out."

"What about that guy you saw in reception a few minutes ago?"

I turned around again to see if anything was happening through the doors - there was no sign of movement now. Had I been mistaken? After all, the light was low and I was shitting myself. I shrugged. "If the mob storm in we'll just have to play it by ear - get out as quick as we can."

"You mean run like girls?"

'Oh, for fuck's sake Gerry, get a grip,' I thought, but we'd both been hardwired not to run from conflict, it was a hard habit to break - even though I thought I'd been doing an okay job with that lately.

"Yeh, that's exactly what we'll do, unless you want in deeper?"

Gerry nodded. I didn't have to point out that, trauma issues or not, it was his arsehole attitude that had landed us here in the first place. Anyway, as we spoke I realised we'd probably both sobered up a good few notches since the fight earlier and that was a bonus. I knew we'd have to stay that way to cope with whatever happened next.

"We better make these our last," I said. Gerry agreed. We sipped our drinks cautiously. I still couldn't stop myself glancing over at those double doors.

Then the music crunched and changed again.

This time it was Garbage, I think I'm *Paranoid*.

'Very funny,' I thought.

8. SECRETS

And the music played on. The dancefloor was even busier now as more and more bodies filtered out from other unseen parts of the Club.

"The girls have been gone a long time," said Gerry. He was right, they had been gone an age.

"Where did they say they were off to?" he asked.

"I don't know - wasn't it the bathroom?"

Could it be they'd brought us in here then just bailed?

But then, as if on perfect cue, the reception doors swung open and both girls walked through. I watched as they skirted around the dance floor, stopping briefly by the DJ booth where Teagan spoke again to the guy on the decks. A few seconds later both were back at our table where they pulled up chairs and sat down.

"Are these ours?" asked Keisha, glancing at the two full glasses of wine, "Thank you, sirs."

Both girls picked up their glasses in unison and sipped at the pale liquid.

"Is everything alright out there?" I asked, tentatively.

"Sorry?" asked Teagan as she looked into my eyes and slowly ran her tongue along her lower lip. I tried not to notice it.

"Out by the front door. I saw a commotion through the glass earlier on - didn't realise you were out there, I thought you'd both gone off to the bathroom?"

"Oh, we did," said Keisha, "But you can walk all the way round to the front door from the toilets without having to come back into the main hall. All these foundation arches, it's a real warren in here..."

"Yeh, in all it's a pretty cool venue," Teagan added with an enthusiastic grin.

"So, there was no trouble?" I asked. I wasn't convinced.

"Oh no," said Keisha, "Well, Vincent did mention some guy tried to barge in earlier - but we're very strict on who we let mingle with us - he was turned around very quickly. It is a private party after all,"

"I know, the barman told us," said Gerry.

"Really? What else did he tell you?" Teagan said, her voice sudden, as if betraying an edge of urgency.

"Well..." started Gerry.

"Not much at all," I cut in. Maybe I was overreacting but I didn't want to start repeating what others had said in the club - could be a recipe for disaster if you didn't know the personal politics and said the wrong thing. If Teagan or Keisha didn't want us to know the full story, that was fine by me. After all, we just needed to be in hiding for a while and if they were prepared to help us out - for whatever reason - I was happy to return the favour by not being nosy.

"There's really no great secret here," said Teagan, "We're all just acquaintances who get together every now and again for a bit of an event." she smiled.

"And we come from all over," continued Keisha, "In fact, depending where the gathering is, there can be someone from just about every corner of the world. This is just a small get together tonight - most of us here are only from around Europe,"

'Okay,' I said. I remembered the map in reception - some kind of guest map maybe?

"So we never really have a meeting in the same city or place twice in a row. It wouldn't be fair on everyone for the sake of travelling."

"Honestly, it feels like years since we were in Scotland - and we *love* this part of town!" smiled Teagan.

"So, what *do* you all have in common then?" Gerry persisted. I threw him an irate look - which he ignored. Again, maybe I was over-reacting, but I *had* hoped he might have worked out that same theory of discretion I had.

"Well, we're all friends for one thing..." offered Keisha. Weak answer.

"Yes, I gathered, but *why* are you all friends?" asked Gerry, "What puts you all together?"

Keisha and Teagan looked at each other as if exchanging thoughts. They kept smiling but it began to look practised. Awkward moment it seemed.

"*Well?*"

"Gerry, please shut up." I said with a smile, "You're beginning to piss everyone off."

He shrugged. There was a short silence at the table punctuated only by the onset of tribal drumming and distinctive guitar riffs - Killing Joke now - really? Good call but another strange choice I thought - or maybe they just liked their alt rock. At that moment I realised almost every track they'd played since we came in had been a favourite of mine at one time or another and that was weird in itself, especially for this part of town where the music was often generic, crowd-pleasing fluff. Teagan gave me a quick look of thanks and turned to Gerry, "It's really not a big deal," she said, "If anything, the main reason is actually a bit dull - it's a genealogy thing."

Our blank looks prompted her further, "Family trees. Everyone here can all trace our genealogy back to a certain time and place that's long gone - so I suppose you could say we're all family in some way. You know, we're not all related but we are loosely connected – and we have some things in common - like a club of sorts. That connection is something we like to hold on to in this day and age,"

Keisha nodded, "And we're a very difficult group to fall in with. In fact, you two should be honoured to be in here, very few outsiders are ever invited into Medusa."

"Yes! But *why?*" said Gerry, smiling, I knew his head was probably fried by what had happened earlier but if this was him attempting cheeky humour then it was the wrong time and place.

"We're also very private in some ways," Keisha said, suddenly icy, "This is our social event, our Nightclub. And if you want to stay and join in - we'll explain as we go." Then she smiled, "I'm sure you wouldn't want to leave too early now would you?" She directed this at Gerry, "Those gents we saw outside did seem very keen to speak to you?"

I leaned over to Gerry and whispered, "What she means, shit-head, is don't ask - then neither will they. Now shut the *fuck* up and just enjoy being safe a little bit longer, okay?"

Gerry got the point. "Okay, sorry. Trying to be funny. I'm an arse." he whined, retreating behind his glass. But to me, Keisha's sudden tone had confirmed it - there was definitely something else going on here, all we could do was hope we wouldn't be dragged into it - whatever it might be. I jumped into the conversation to try and change the subject, "The barman said you do food at your parties too - sounded like a big deal?"

"Oh, yes - that's the whole point of the night really," said Keisha, all traces of iciness now gone. "A good wholesome, all round evening's entertainment really, just like the music - something for everyone,"

"As we said, if you'd like to stay, you're most welcome to join us for what's left of the night?" asked Teagan.

"Sure - of course," I said, putting on my bravest face.

"Do you often eat so late though?" Gerry asked.

"Yes – it might seem strange for us Brits but most other cultures eat later in the evening anyway and some of the guests aren't acclimatised to being a few hours behind yet. It just seems easier to go with what they're used to, so we let them set the pace."

"Again, it's just being fair to everyone," said Keisha.

Complete bullshit answer, I thought.

"It *is* a bit of a fucking drag though, I'm famished..." deadpanned Teagan. She caught Keisha's eye and both burst into a fit of girlish giggles which belied their vampish looks. Gerry looked at me as if asking for approval to converse again after his verbal time out. I shrugged and rolled my eyes. We were absolutely in a world of shit on the outside and I was pretty sure we were being lied to - but maybe I *was* being overly paranoid. We did need to leave - but a few more minutes surely wouldn't hurt. Deal with all the bad stuff later, right?

And so, with the ice broken and only a few minor stalls, we all began easily chatting. It was bizarre. As the conversation turned to our backgrounds we found out about the monotony of Keisha's job as an Actuary in London and Teagan's medical studies in Dublin, which she financed by working the evenings as a private hire driver. Suddenly they both seemed very easy company. When it came to our turn, both Gerry and I gave them our rehearsed and vague back stories about having been squaddies once upon a time, then happily returning to civvy life with no issues - thankfully neither girl pushed or questioned any of it.

As we talked though, I noticed the girls seemed to want to up the pace of the drinking. Was that a bad thing? Yes it was. All my best laid plans of staying sharp and leaving were soon by the wayside as I surmised they must have had some kind of eye contact going with the barman, who seemed to magically appear every time the levels in our glasses dropped. This felt surreal - we had both been through a horrific trauma that night, yet here we were drinking and chatting with a couple of new friends just as if none of it had happened. I knew it was wrong - or sick - or something - but I wasn't complaining, there was no point. Just get the fuck on with it. Maybe I only wanted to delay the inevitable when we left.

As we drank, talked and laughed, time rolled on and the music began to change much more seamlessly than earlier - from the sounds of Garbage and Killing Joke to Morissette to Sinatra to Nirvana by way of Bobby Goldsboro and P.J. Harvey - Bauhaus via Linkin Park, Britney and Siouxsie - diverse was too mild a word for it. In some ways the playlist seemed to add to the ease of being there for me, it was all so familiar. I guessed the DJ was probably on some kind of psychedelics but in those strange surroundings, to my drunk and whacked out ears it all made musical sense. And I still knew every song. Weird? Yes it was - but I listen to all kinds of music - so probably just happy coincidence. Maybe all these folks were just on my wavelength? When I pushed her on it, Teagan explained that everyone brought some music of their own (CDs or vinyl only) as well as a bottle of their favourite wine (preferably to complement the food) - so the eclectic playlist was mostly down to a nominated DJ trying to make it work on hired equipment with a whole bunch of music they may not be familiar with. Sounded plausible, if slightly on the lame side.

But as the time passed and the wine began to dull everything further, I realised my own guard was beginning to drop - and strangely, I found I didn't care. What was done was done – what lay ahead was in the future, right? Somehow, the reluctance I'd had about this club, the bad vibes, the nagging feeling that something wasn't right - they were all gradually wearing away. I also couldn't help but notice that Gerry seemed to be getting on very well with Teagan – not just in a 'successfully chatted her up' way, but as if they were connecting really well – as if they were actually on each other's wavelengths - weird though that may be, knowing Gerry. Who knew? If nothing else good came from this tonight, then maybe he'd finally found someone who was a foil for his demons? It was a thought.

I asked Keisha about the name. "So why Medusa? Is there a story there?"

"Ha, yes," she laughed, "Well firstly, some of the Olds here claim to be able to trace their roots as far back as Marco Polo's days, to a tribe of Sumatrans, believe it or not, who were apparently quite notorious at the time, so I gather,"

"In what way?"

"Umm, I couldn't really say... You know what *all* Olds are like with their secrets, not very forthcoming around us youngsters, so we just enjoy the social side and leave the dusty stuff to them."

"Okay, I get that – but why Medusa?"

"Oh, I know this!" said Teagan, "There's an old painting in The Louvre…"

"Yes, 'The Raft of the Medusa.' There was disaster at sea about two hundred years ago, a ship called the Medusa sank and - from what they tell us - most of the Olds in the Club can trace their ancestry back to surviving on the raft after the shipwreck," said Keisha.

"So," said Teagan, "This disaster was awful and a real scandal in its day. The Captain was blamed for the sinking and most of the crew died. The ones who survived lived through all sorts of horrors and to make things worse, they were very harshly judged afterwards. So this Club was started in secret as the people of the day were, err - less than understanding. But the whole thing has just kept going - and even though it's a closely guarded secret, we still keep gaining new members. We both think that's probably because of the way the world is today,"

"The way *people* are today," said Keisha

What the fuck? That wasn't a clear answer in anyone's books. It probably raised even more questions if anything - but her eyes told me she was finished on the subject so I decided to leave it at that. If that was all she was saying, then that was fine.

"All sounds a bit like the bloody Masons to me," smiled Gerry.

"Honestly," said Keisha, "There's nothing unnatural going on here, we're all quite open - to certain people. The exclusive side is more to do with everyone's privacy and carrying on traditions and heritage,"

"And all of that is way too dull and philosophical for banter at a disco, believe me. But you're not too far off the mark, what's that tagline the Masons have these days? Not a secret society - but a society with secrets?"

She sounded vaguely patronising, as if she were trying to make out the whole idea was above our heads. Okay, fine. And for the record, 'unnatural' was a strange choice of word.

"I see..." I said, maybe a little too slowly, "Maybe a chat for another time then,"

Keisha smiled, "Okay, later then," as her eyes lingered on mine longer than they maybe should have. I shifted uncomfortably in my seat, I wasn't quite sure where all this was leading now.

9. GONE

By now the aroma of freshly cooked food was in the air. The smell made me realise how long it was since I'd last eaten and my stomach began to anticipate the thought of doing so again. My eye was drawn to someone approaching the table, a distinguished middle-aged man in a dark suit and tie. He stood behind the remaining empty chair which creaked as he rested his hands on its back. As they closed around the wood I noticed his fingernails were manicured into fine points.

"May I?" he asked, his eyes trawling slowly around us.

"Of course, Pierre," said Keisha. The man sat down and clasped his hands on the table in front of him with the seasoned air of a TV news presenter. He smiled looking all around the table as Keisha introduced him, "Gerry, Paul, this is Pierre, he's our trusty organiser. He's also the executive head chef and wine buyer - it's him you really have to thank for all this hospitality tonight," Pierre nodded an acknowledgement to us both. We both graciously nodded back.

"Good evening my friends," Pierre said in a deep, dramatic tone which, like the barman's earlier, sounded put on, "The girls here have already told me about you - good of you to join us so late in the evening!"

Jesus, this gets weirder every minute, I thought.

"Oh, it's our pleasure, honestly," I said, somewhat lamely. This was really becoming a bit too much - if all these people *were* playing some kind of charade then Pierre's pretence and pointy manicure were enough to edge me over into plain pissed off territory. I wasn't sure how much more of this patronising drama I could take, private party or not. I also couldn't help but notice Pierre's dark eyes lingering over both Gerry and me for longer than I thought was polite.

"Please forgive my intrusion, I just wanted to let you know *personally* that the next course will be served within the next few minutes." Keisha and Teagan both grinned widely.

"Superb!" Keisha beamed. The girls were like putty in his hands - he was obviously one of the top dogs here.

His brief act over, Pierre stood up and smoothly walked off into the lights and clamour of the dance floor leaving Gerry and me watching his departure with vaguely puzzled looks.

"Pierre doesn't sound very French to me," Gerry said, eventually.

"Oh, but he is," said Teagan, "He was born in France and came to this country when he was young. He went to one of the most exclusive schools in the Highlands somewhere, so... err…" she faltered, "…I suppose he won't have much of an accent left. But he really is wonderful at organising these nights for us. He has all the best connections and ideas and he's always willing to throw in a few surprises!" At that, the music faded and the muffled voice of the DJ was heard for the first time through the speaker system.

"Ladies and Gentlemen, umm - it's my pleasure to announce that the next course is now being served."

Then the lights came up - but that wasn't saying much. The extra brightness only went far enough to lighten the middle of the room, leaving most of the outlying snugs and alcoves still shrouded in shadow. The girls stood up and began making their way to the buffet table at the far side of the room - we quickly followed them. Complete strangers smiled and nodded at us on our way as we joined the short queue leading to the table.

The table itself was lit by a square, overhanging box light which looked as if it may have served over a snooker or pool table in a previous life - but the spread it illuminated was exquisite. From where I stood I could see that when it came to feeding themselves, these people, whoever they were, spared no expense. There were no sausage rolls or hurriedly defrosted vol-au-vents here.

My stomach felt empty as my eyes took in beautifully presented selections of thinly cut cooked meats, smooth and coarse, red and white with selections of salads, fruit and bread and an assortment of bowls filled with thick, dark dips and sauces. Not being much of a foodie myself I could only have guessed at what half this stuff might have been - but it looked and smelled delicious. Between the exertion of our earlier experience and the steady flow of wine through the evening, I found I was now almost ravenous with hunger.

Then Gerry tapped me on the shoulder, "Hey - see those two guys helping themselves to that venison type stuff up ahead?" he asked, pointing to two well-dressed thirtysomethings, in the midst of filling their plates.

"I see them,"

"I recognise them. I'm pretty sure they're doctors - or something - from the hospital,"

"Really? Are you sure?"

"Yeh - well, fairly. They look familiar - I wouldn't know their names but, well, you know what it's like in my job with different faces all day."

"Do you think they might be able to shed any light on this lot?"

"Dunno. I'll rack my brains and see if I can't remember where they're from. See if I can think of some way to start some sort of chat with them without getting their backs up."

You'd be lucky, I thought.

The queue moved quickly and I watched the girls, following their lead. They moved eagerly and expertly as if they knew the food, garnishing each with particular vegetables and sauces. I took similar choices and combinations onto my own plate – I didn't want to look too much like a novice.

Our food selected, we returned to the table to find yet another bottle of Chardonnay opened for us there. Shit.

As we sat and began to eat, I caught sight of Pierre standing by a distant doorway watching keenly over the proceedings with a grin. He caught sight of me watching him and smiled back, his expression never faltering.

"This is pretty good," I heard Gerry say, through a mouthful of half chewed meat.

"What?" I turned back round to our own company.

"The food..." said Gerry, "...it's good."

"Oh, right," I whispered, "Best enjoy it, we're going to have a long weekend when we get out of here,"

"Oh, give me a break," he moaned. He was right though; the food was delicious.

Both girls ate silently, as if in reverence, clearing almost everything from their plates before passing any comment.

"Excellent, good old Pierre, up to his usual standards!" said Keisha. Teagan smiled and nodded in delighted agreement between sips of wine.

After a while, our empty plates were collected by a group of jovial older women and men who scurried around the tables looking vaguely surreal in ill-fitting waiters' and maids' outfits. They were all wearing half face, white masks similar to the full face one I'd seen outside the Club earlier with the paint smears across the eyes. They removed all the plates and cutlery from around the room with breathtaking speed and efficiency then wiped down all the surfaces with cloths that smelled of lemon and disinfectant. It all appeared very thorough, very swift. Then just as we began some more small talk with the girls, the DJ cranked the music back on with raucous meanderings I recognised straight away as being early Radiohead. What *was* that guy singing - an *airbag* saved his life? I'd always wondered, never checked. Why was I even thinking that? The alcohol was sending my mind off in tangents...

Gerry dabbed his mouth with a napkin obviously trying to make a good impression, then placed it atop a pile of plates being collected by our own maid. She looked at us all in turn – she was smiling, but the mask over her upper face only made her look blank and disturbing. Then, with a stack of dishes in hand, she paused and began chatting to the girls about all the best sights to see while they were in town, the Castle, the Museum, the Cove at Gilmerton especially, Mary Kings Close and a few others I didn't quite catch. Gerry leaned over towards me and spoke quietly, "You know, I think I do know where I've seen those guys before," he said. But Teagan's ears pricked up at this and she broke away from her chat with the maid, "Oh - you've seen someone here you know?" she asked excitedly.

Gerry turned to her, "Well, I *think* I might - remember I told you I worked in the hospital? Well, I thought I saw a couple of the medical guys in here who work in the wards. Wasn't quite sure where at first, but I think it's finally come to me..." Both girls were now eagerly sitting forward and seemed to be hanging onto his every word. Gerry looked taken aback by their interest.

"Uh, I usually see them when I take the patients into theatre, I'm pretty sure they're anaesthetists,"

"Really!" said Keisha, looking excitedly at Teagan. Teagan turned back round to Gerry.

"Well, we do know most of the people who come to these nights, but we don't always know about their day work. Why don't we go over and speak to them?" she said, "Imagine not knowing something like that," She turned to Keisha, "Would you look after Paul while we're gone, sweetie?" Something unspoken seemed to pass between the two girls as they smiled at each other. Keisha looked over at me and moistened her lips with her tiny tongue. I felt that somehow, even through the haze of the strong wine, the evening's events had just taken yet another strange turn.

"Of course, I'd *love* to..." said Keisha - too slowly, too deliberately.

"Come on Gerry, let's have a wander around," said Teagan as she stood up and began moving towards the dance floor. Gerry stood up, helping her move her own chair out the way in a mock gentlemanly manner. Despite everything I could tell just by the way he moved around her that he seemed enraptured - in his mind he had probably scored big time but I did hope there might be something more there.

"So, did you see where your friends went?" I heard Teagan ask as she led him off into the strobe lights.

"No, I can't see them now, they must be sitting in the dark somewhere..." their voices merged into the music and then became lost. I saw Teagan turn to him - then she took his hand and both disappeared off into the crowded alcoves and recesses.

10. PROMISE

"Maybe you'd like a little more wine?" Keisha purred. She was looking at me differently now, her eyes seductively narrow, her lips parted and glistening. Before I could answer she was already pouring more strong, pale drink into my glass. I nodded dumbly, I wasn't in much of a mind to argue anymore; the slow intoxication of strong wine, good food and attractive female company had already skewed my sensibility, even though it went against everything I'd ever learned. Although my mind had been mostly focussed on staying out of harm's way since it happened, that pointless, stupid fight had really shaken me and it had drawn a strong line of unease through everything that had happened since. I was still worried about Gerry too, he'd been freaked earlier, he still wasn't out of the woods yet and now I'd lost sight of him in this dark, disorienting place.

I also hadn't been able to shake the feeling of dread at our imminent involvement with the law, both civilian and military which I knew would be blindsiding us soon. But despite everything, I found I was pushing all that out of my head just to be there with Keisha in that moment. It was plain from the outset these girls were charismatic and attractive, but it wasn't until I found myself close enough to inhale her perfume that I realised I'd become utterly spellbound by Keisha's enticing air of almost aggressive sex. As I thought clearly for the first time about the possibility of fucking with her, I realised I was probably far enough gone to do anything she might ask of me just to be able to take things that far. I mean, my whole future was probably screwed now anyway, why not just screw it up some more?

She slid her chair along the floor, closer to my side. As she did so I realised I could sense her above all the other sweet sensations in the room. My stomach fluttered as she reached over and stroked the inside of my leg through my jeans. "You know what? I think we could end up being *really* close friends, you and I," she whispered. I looked into her eyes and they seemed aglow. I felt stirring between my legs.

(No - damn, something else - not right now - one thing was going to stop all this.)

"Well... did you enjoy the meal?" she whispered slowly, in close to me - I felt my head rush, stirred by her warm breath at my ear.

(Christ no - I knew I was going to blow it - I couldn't help myself.)

"Yes..." I was already beginning to feel stupid, angry at myself for having to ruin the moment before I even mentioned it.

"I'm *so* glad we met, you know..."

(No, I couldn't put it off any longer...)

"So am I -" I was cut short as I felt the warm softness of her tongue as she leaned in close and lightly teased it along my earlobe, my whole body tingled as I felt the moist trail on my skin cool under her breath...

(Oh God, here goes...)

"Keisha - I'm *really* sorry but I'm going to have to leave you for a few seconds."

"Ohhh?" she complained, breathily in my ear. I sighed, hating myself for it - it was so typically me.

"Could you tell me where the Gents bathroom is?"

To my relief, she leaned back slightly and chuckled. Under the table her hand moved slowly over my leg to squeeze my hand in turn. "Of course," she smiled, "I totally understand - if you've gotta go..."

I gave her an apologetic smile. With conflicting sensations of discomfort and longing in my groin, I could clearly feel my want for this girl overtaking every other thought I had -and that sort of thing never happened to me. Nevertheless, she seemed oblivious to my poor timing and her eyes remained fixed on mine even though she knew I had just blown the flow.

"You would be quickest going through those double doors and then turn to the left - you'll see it just a little way along that corridor," she said, "There's a sign,"

"Thanks."

"You won't be long, will you?"

"No way,"

"Good," she smiled, "And don't get lost."

"Don't worry - just hold that thought,"

"I will. And I mean it - some of this place... Well, it's a bit dark and dangerous in parts and I'm afraid Pierre doesn't care much for Health and Safety..."

I nodded, smiled and tore myself away from her gaze, breaking off the touch of our hands as I stood up and walked towards the doors. Until that moment I hadn't even realised we'd been holding hands.

I walked across the empty dance floor (I guess Radiohead had never really been floor fillers) and was again thrown occasional waves and smiles from strangers who happened to catch my eye. I did my best to return the acknowledgements even though it felt wrong.

There was so much going on in my head right then - between the alcohol, the food, the atmosphere in the Club and that surge of lust for Keisha which had surprised and overtaken me, everything seemed to have meshed to create some sort of sudden, intoxicating euphoria for life and the moment. By then I'd almost lost sight of why I was in their Club in the first place - I was beginning to feel as if nothing else mattered.

I opened the double doors and glanced back, only to see that in my absence Pierre had scuttled straight over to Keisha and was now stooped down, talking in her ear. Keisha was nodding sporadically as if agreeing with different points. I shrugged it off, turned around and saw Vincent, the doorman we met earlier, standing sentry in a corner of the reception area brooding in the ultraviolet light. I nodded to him - he acknowledged me with the least possible effort and continued to stand impassively as if in a time and space all of his own, waiting for the next distraction from this world to intrude.

I followed Keisha's directions and turned left, walking a few yards down a musty corridor where the light bulbs seemed to have failed. Behind me I heard Radiohead fade and the upbeat chords of another track begin - I couldn't hear exactly what it was though as the doors were now closed and all I could hear was the beat.

A few paces along the curved passageway I saw a distempered wooden door with an A4 piece of paper pinned to the top panel, it read, "Gentlemen's Bathroom" in the fanciful flourish of a calligrapher. Someone certainly cared about the occasion of taking a piss, I thought.

I pushed the door open to find the room aglow with flickering light from countless candles, tealights and incense sticks standing in glasses, melted on to bottle tops and carefully arranged around the flat surfaces in the room. It was pretty impressive - a soft and relaxing chillout after the strobes and glare of the Club. But in the gentle glow I could still see a line of badly stained urinals and a couple of toilet cubicles with the doors broken on their hinges. I realised also that even through the pleasant must of the incense, there was a sharp tang of sewage in the air. Seemed like someone had done their best to overwrite the smell. The candlelight reflected warmly against the far wall where a row of mirrors hung over the wash-hand basins. This might have been a decent bathroom at one time but now it was seriously neglected however hard you tried to mask it. Still, the place had a calming and strangely comforting effect and I suppose Pierre wouldn't have had time to fix everything.

I made for the nearest urinal bowl and began to empty my bladder in relief. I stood and slowed my breath as the liquid filtered out, shaking off some of that drink fuelled compliance I'd felt with Keisha earlier as the discomfort inside released. Jeez, what had I been thinking? I'd never been in so much deep shit since the last time I'd worn a uniform - everything was properly messing with my head. This whole place was the opposite of what we'd seen earlier in the Bank Bar - everyone was so forthcoming, so accepting - yet I was none the wiser as to what was really going on. I remembered how uneasy I'd felt just before we stepped through those doors, even though the place had been a godsend at the time. But it all just seemed *too* good - *too* lucky - and that's just not me, not by a long shot. Also, our companions, enigmatic and beautiful though they were, still hadn't come close to offering any decent explanation for this 'private party'. I shook my head slowly and felt my mind swirl heavily inside. This was no dream, it was all happening sure as I was standing there pissing, but it didn't add up - and that stuck like a shard in my mind.

So even if I was grateful for all the sanctuary and hospitality, I decided an accidental wrong turn or two in the name of exploration might just have to be in order before I re-joined Keisha, even if only to put my mind at rest.

11. SERVED

As soon as I'd finished I buttoned up my jeans and turned to wash my hands in a basin which looked grimy, even in the candlelight. I picked up a bar of soap from the basin top, couldn't summon any hot water so I resigned myself to using the cold. I winced as the freezing water poured between my fingers - but it sent a refreshing shiver through my body. Without any further thought I doused my face with it, hoping the sudden cold might just help shake off some of the intoxication and weirdness I was feeling. The effect was limited - the sensation rippled through me - the sudden drop in temperature was bracing and it did help - but my mind still felt clouded. I pondered the situation as I watched my cold, dripping features in the mirror.

But then, for the briefest of moments, the distant pulse of the disco was overwritten by a sudden, muffled shriek, which - if my sense of direction was still reliable - sounded as if it had come directly from beyond the wall in front of me. It had been a swift, sharp cry, but distinct enough. I was sure I hadn't imagined it. I turned my ear to the wall, straining to hear if I could pick anything else out. And there it was again - I clearly heard it a second time - shorter, more of a gasp the second time. As before, it was as if the noise was coming from the next room just beyond the mirrored wall. Well, my guts had been telling me all night something odd was going on in that place - I decided now was the time to go and take a look.

Shaking the water off my face I stepped out of the bathroom and brusquely glanced up and down the corridor. The smell of cooked food was much stronger here than in the Club so presumably this meant I was closer to the kitchen. The passage outside the bathroom door curved away in both directions from where I stood and I guessed it may have circled widely all the way around the main section of the Club. The main entrance door and reception were beyond my line of sight and I judged that if anyone were to leave this bathroom and walk the other way, they would quickly vanish into the dark and probably not be missed by Vincent, who seemed oblivious to everything last time I saw him. I closed the door as quietly as I could and walked down the corridor to the right to where - presumably - any access for that next room might be.

A few yards on, I saw the outline of a door in the wall, its surface was cold, smooth and metallic like stainless steel - presumably this was it. I pressed my ear up against the metal and listened carefully. There were muffled voices beyond it - the difference in pitch told me there was at least one male and one female talking on the other side - but the door seemed too thick and heavy to afford any clarity. The talking was punctuated by short outbursts of laughter and grunts of exertion, as if some couple were either having great fun lifting something heavy - or getting frisky with each other. I quietly twisted the door handle - it wouldn't budge. Shit.

Just then I heard a sudden outpour of voices behind me in the reception area. I released the handle and backed off further down the corridor into the dark to get out of view, praying no one was going to walk my way. I held my breath as a brief and loud conversation passed between two girls about where the hell that arsehole barman had gone, just when he was needed most.

I exhaled slowly as I heard the voices carry off in the other direction. I presumed from the symmetry in the corridor that if the Gents's bathroom was in this section; then the Ladies would most likely be down the other - I assumed that's where they must have gone.

I stepped back to the outer wall and flanked further round into the darkness, wondering if that room might have another way in - after all, this had all probably been part of the same cellar at one time and Keisha said herself the place was like a warren. Maybe they had interconnecting doors - rooms inside leading to other rooms? With every step the light seemed to become less pronounced and the outlines less distinct - but I moved slowly and my eyes seemed to adjust surprisingly quickly. I soon found I could make out vague shapes in the gloom. I stole a glance behind - if anyone were to use that bathroom now, they would most likely spot me lurking in the dark and I'd be busted - so far though, the corridor seemed clear.

After maybe twenty feet or so of feeling my way along brick and plaster walls, I felt a different texture - the raised wood of what seemed like a door surround. My fingers edged around the corner and passed over external metal hinges - this was clearly another door. I placed my ear against it for a few seconds and held my breath. There were no sounds beyond, only the distant thump of music from the Club and the occasional impressions of voices and laughter in the next room down - whatever was happening in there was clearly still going on. I peered into the dark grey around the door and could just make out some detail - there was no handle on this door, just a 'push' plate. I applied some pressure and found the door gave easily, opening inwards and releasing a faint stream of light from inside the room. I quickly slipped through the doorway and supported the door, letting it swing gently closed behind me. A spring murmured as it travelled further out than the surround suggested it would and I realised it must have been mounted on double hinges with no stops to hold it - a two-way swing door - probably a main egress from the kitchen.

Inside the smell of food was even stronger, a sharp mix of garlic, onions and cooking steaks. I stood awkwardly against the wall and looked around the room. It was a sparse affair, and like the bathroom earlier it was lit by several large burning candle stubs melted onto the tops of empty bottles. The only furniture in the room was a small, wooden dining table and grey swivel chair set against the farthest wall. On the table lay an open box of candles and a few matchboxes, their contents littered beside a pile of papers clamped with bulldog clips. A large buttoned pocket calculator and some pens lay strewn about the desk as if it was some kind of admin base.

I walked quietly over and leafed through some of the notes. They were what I would have expected – receipts for wine, local vegetable supply, the hire of disco equipment, lights and the temporary dance-floor – basically the whole party as far as I could see; no surprises there. I held the bundle of papers under the candlelight and saw more detail - most had been signed by the purchaser but there were a whole bunch of different names on the agreements - and all had similar indecipherable handwriting. Didn't Keisha say that Pierre had organised all this himself? There was no sign of any Pierre in all this admin. I looked closer, trying to make out some of the scrawled autographs in the dim lighting and began to see names suggesting themselves: Mr Dahmer, Mr Sutcliff, Mr Nilsson - I knew those names somehow - those guys were all killers of some sort, right? It seemed as if the organiser wasn't keen on giving out real names and probably trying to pass some kind of black humour in the process.

"Sick bastards," I muttered aloud.

I pulled a few candles out of the box and stuffed them in my jacket pocket along with a handful of matches - I thought they might come in useful.

Looking around the room the only other features I could see were two dark jackets hanging on a row of coat hooks on to the far wall and also a door in the wall adjacent, which by its position looked as if may connect to the area behind the wall in the bathroom. Crossing to the coat-hooks my stomach did a turn as I saw both were black flying jackets with 'Lady's' embroidered on the front. These were just like the jackets worn by the bouncers chasing our tails earlier - were those bastards down here in the Club? Could they all be in this together? Could it be the girls were only holding us there till they gathered their friends to pulp us? Maybe. *Shite!*

I decided it was time to leave; the only mission now was to find Gerry and get out, whether we were on the promise of pretty girls or not.

But just at that moment, I heard a playful female drawl from behind the connecting door, "...but you know I *so like* to do it this way!" It was unmistakably Teagan's. I reasoned that if Teagan was in there, then so was Gerry - well, I was just going to have to interrupt.

I strode over to the doorway but just as I reached out to grip the handle, the door swung suddenly outwards, forced open by the burly frame of the Barman we'd met earlier. I jumped back to get out of the door's arc and saw he was carefully wiping the area around the corners of his mouth with a bloodied handkerchief. Had he hurt himself? Had somebody thumped him?

He looked at me as if surprised, then recovered himself and grinned widely, "Oh, I wouldn't go in there, sir," he said, quickly folding the handkerchief. As I held his gaze I saw his eyes were open just slightly wider than they should be, his pupils maybe just a bit *too* dilated even in the low light. There was something way more sinister to this guy than just that congenially polite exterior.

He must have read my intention before I moved as he stepped out of the doorframe and blocked me, slamming the door shut so hard that he sent himself spinning sideways in the process. I swiftly threw myself into the gap between his body and the frame, brushing quickly past his bulk and sending him off balance in the process - which put me directly in front of the door.

In that sudden movement he lost grip of the handkerchief – I saw it fall to the floor where it landed with an unpleasant, wet sound. I grabbed the door handle but before I could pull it open, I felt his arm lock around my neck from behind and haul me viciously backwards.

"I told you - I *wouldn't* go in there!" This time his voice was heavy with threat. I jabbed back hard with my elbow and felt the blow connect solidly near the middle of his ribcage. The pressure around my throat dropped as the Barman stumbled and released his grip, unbalanced and gasping. He landed clumsily and rolled - probably winded - but I knew I had to move quickly now.

I pulled the door open and stepped into the next room which was a much bigger and brighter space. I squinted - the sudden glare of stark florescent light and white tiled walls after the candlelit bathroom was dazzling. The smell of sweet, raw meat and cooking vegetables in here was overpowering - this was the kitchen.

The room was a good size and it was lined with heavy looking steel worktops and benches. The surfaces around the room were littered - as I would have expected - with arrangements of food in various states of preparation, obviously laid out and waiting their turn to be served up in the next course. A stack of black and blue plastic bags overflowed with empty containers and waste piled up next to the farthest away door. On a grid of industrial gas stoves,

I saw steam rising from large steel pots where vegetables simmered and bobbed over the edges.

In the centre of the room were two freestanding metal trolleys, each supporting the remains of a large butchered carcass. The nearest seemed to be an entire skeleton side of beef; some unfortunate piece of cattle expertly picked and carved almost clean by a team of butchers. But as I took a careful step towards the carcass I realised the ribs were far too small for the type of beast they must surely have belonged to. I drew closer and saw the upper part of the meat was covered with a torn plastic bag weighed down at either side with piles of curved and cleanly picked bones, some still linked by sinuous strands. It wasn't until I was close enough to fully see the proportions of the carcass that I realised - this was no piece of dead cattle; these remains were human.

Something inside wanted me to be sure. I reached over and - at full arm's length - slowly lifted the weighted piece of plastic away, exposing the head of the carcass. In that moment, every horror in my past, everything I thought I'd processed, shaken off and rationalised welled up in my head when I saw what lay underneath. Only part of the face remained, most of what was visible under a layer of dark, congealing blood and matter was the exposed bone of the skull, its empty eye socket peering lifelessly up at the underside of the bag. What remained of the flesh had been neatly carved away from a point just below the chin to reveal features vaguely familiar to me from much earlier in the night. Numbly, I realised this was the owner of one of the jackets hanging on the pegs in the room next door – this was what remained of the doorman who ran after us just as Keisha and Teagan ushered us down into the Club. Except that now, most of his skin, muscle and flesh had been picked, peeled and scraped from his bones. I recoiled from the table, only to see there was another stripped carcass stacked neatly on the steel shelf underneath.

There was a sudden ringing clatter as my heel glanced off the side of a metal bucket on the floor. As I stumbled back I felt the contents spill out, splashing my boots, soaking warmly through the material of my jeans. When I looked down, the gory sight and stench of spilt blood, folded innards and discarded eyeballs assaulted all of my senses in one full battery.

I felt my stomach begin to heave - but a further shock denied me the luxury of being sick. On hearing the metallic clatter, a familiar face suddenly shot up from the sliced mess of bone, flesh and gristle on the next trolley down. I realised I had been so wrapped up in the revulsion and shock of the first trolley that despite its closeness, I'd barely paid any attention to the second.

And in that moment, I realised the carcass on the second table was Gerry - his face still easily recognisable with most of the skin still in place, except for his lower lip and the exposed bone around his jawline. The head that suddenly appeared amidst his bones was that of Teagan. As she drew herself slowly upwards I saw she was naked - at least to her waist - and she was holding what looked like the missing piece of flesh from Gerry's face in her mouth, excess blood trickling gruesomely down her chest and belly. There were roughly smeared red stripes across her face at eye level - presumably blood - which gave her an aggressive, tribal appearance - the same markings I'd seen on the mask on the wall outside the Club. It looked as if she had been lying or squatting low alongside Gerry's stripped body in amongst the gore and residue.

With her eyes now on me she spat out the flapping remains, pouted and smiled teasingly, arching her back slightly to accentuate the swell of her breasts - the trail of blood now looking somehow perversely erotic as it flowed downwards.

"Mmmm… It *is* an acquired taste, but so gorgeous raw," she said slowly. Metal glinted as she raised a small carving knife and nimbly sliced a thin strip of flesh from Gerry's frontage. She held my gaze as the meat snagged in coming away from his chest where the nipple held fast - then looking down with an air of indifference, she flashed the blade again and sliced through the offending piece of meat.

I was rooted to the spot in revulsion and fear.

"Oh, come on," she said enticingly, "Don't look so shocked - you enjoyed your enemies a little while ago - wouldn't a friend taste even *better*?"

I began to feel the room move around me - my head spun with the horror of this and everything before. Despite everything I knew about self-preservation, I probably would have passed out on the spot had I not heard the approaching shuffle of the Barman's feet behind me. Then I remembered the blood I'd seen him dabbing away from around his mouth - and realised he was probably in on all this carnage with the rest of them. With all the energy I could muster I forced everything from my head - to deal with all this I had to be something I wasn't anymore. I took a sharp breath in and, lashing out with my clenched fist, I spun around and caught the Barman on his approach, the punch connecting fully in his face. I felt skin split under my knuckles as I connected somewhere around his nose, jolting his head suddenly backwards and his glasses flying into the air - a direct hit. I saw in an instant he was going down. As he landed I took a wide step over him towards the door - only to see it pull away from me as I reached out for the handle. As the door opened to allow the light to spill out from my room I saw it fall on the hard features of Vincent, the Medusa Doorman, who was now standing immediately in front of me beyond the doorway.

In the instant it took Vincent to process what was happening, I launched myself directly at him, knowing I had to take him down quick. But the sudden, instinctive push caused my balance to waver and I toppled forwards into him, my head connecting solidly with the area above his stomach. Luckily, the way I had fallen had shifted all my weight into the lunge - he reeled and fell with the impact, buckling with the sudden winding. Lucky shot - but I was down too. For a brief moment we all lay dazed on the floor between the two rooms writhing in pains of one sort or another.

Then - probably because I was the most terrified - I regained myself, vaulted up and launched myself through the kitchen doorway, over Vincent's folding body and into the admin room beyond. I paused for a second to glance back to the kitchen only to see that Teagan was now completely gone with it all. She had returned to sprawling amongst Gerry's remains and had unashamedly taken to removing more of his flesh, working it with her knife and mouth. I couldn't watch any further.

I bolted across the room and out of the far door back into the gloomy corridor where I'd stood only minutes earlier, blissfully unaware of what lay ahead. The relief of bursting out of those rooms was overwhelming, like escaping from some vivid, vile nightmare - except I knew I hadn't actually escaped yet. And - Gerry was dead - murdered by these people for nothing more than...

I realised my clarity was going, images were beginning to seep through my thoughts, other awful things locked in my memory that, strangely, had nothing to do with this place. The remains of the usual voice inside my head made me wonder if all the bad things I'd managed to block over the years had been released by those horrors in the kitchen. I could see them all - tangles of massacred civilians in pits - butchered soldiers, no more than kids -blood soaking into the sand in the ringing aftermath of exploded landmines... And then Gerry, lying dead in the next room – to the moment in the desert when those girls realised they were going to die and began to scream, those final howls of anguish before everything stopped forever...

I had to survive this.

I inhaled deep - seize on it all - use the anger - use the hurt.

'Focus you idiot, *focus*!' I exhaled and forced everything out of my head - there was only one single objective now: escape, live through this.

The darkness in the corridor was disorienting after the stark light of the kitchen but I knew I wasn't far from the front doorway, which would presumably now be unguarded. I decided it would be my best way out. I bolted along the corridor towards the ultraviolet glow. Turning the corner, I saw there was no one there. My heart lifted as I saw the bar across the front door looked insecure, as if it had just been laid over the fixings with nothing to lock it in place. But just as I was about to vault the final steps and haul the bar back, the double doors of the Club were thrown open by Pierre who immediately stopped in his tracks to glare at me. The look on my face could only have told him the secret was out. He snarled like an animal, baring his teeth and began stalking towards me, hands poised and wavering like snakes and forming claws tipped by those sharpened nails I'd seen earlier - he was ready to slice.

I had to move fast and there were precious few options. Even though they looked flimsy, I grabbed hold of the closest of the wooden chairs at the desk and charged at him full on with the legs raised out front. As soon as the wood connected with him I felt his strength as he pushed back hard - but I managed to get enough momentum into it to slam him hard against the doors behind. It wasn't enough to put him down but he was off balance and stilled, if only for a few brief seconds. He'd be up in seconds so there was no time to work on moving the bar - it looked as if the only way out of the reception area was the way I had come. I spun around, vaulting off back into the corridor, hoping neither Vincent nor the Barman had recovered enough to get themselves back out of that room yet. With as much strength as I could find I broke into a run. Within a few seconds I reached the door to the kitchen anteroom and just as I passed I saw it begin to slowly draw open. I dug in deeper and as I passed I resisted all temptation to look inside, focusing instead on the darkness of the corridor ahead, praying it would lead to some other way out.

12. FLIGHT

I hadn't covered as much ground as I'd wanted to before I lost all semblance of light. For the first time I began to regret not having a mobile phone, even if only for the torch. My run had now slowed to more of a cautious walk and the only thing around me now was a sense of overwhelming blackness and the sound of my own movement reflecting back at me. I began to feel my way forward with my fingers along the walls, trying to avoid tripping by carefully pushing my toes out and forward with every step. I knew this was dangerous, moving deeper into a place I couldn't map or be sure of retracing my steps from - but at that moment there were no other options.

The seconds turned to over a minute and the open corridor appeared to change into a series of connected chambers. By that time, I realised I could only have seen a fraction of the floorspace inside the building. It was probably safe to assume this cellar level sprawled the entire footprint of the building which, from what I could remember from outside, was substantial. But in the dead gloom my eyes seemed to adjust surprisingly quickly. It was odd as I wasn't aware of any light source, but I realised I

was beginning to pick out vague shapes in the dark –
openings in walls, rubble piles, ridges underfoot where the
floor was uneven. Somehow it was becoming easier to
judge distances and to see whether the archways which
punctuated the walls were either cellar alcoves or openings
to other areas. I reasoned this could only have been the
adrenaline boosting my senses in this heightened state.

I stopped and stilled myself to listen for any sounds of
pursuit - there were none, or at least none yet. I'd been in
some sick situations over the years but nothing like this.
Even so, I knew only too well how these scenarios worked -
I knew what I'd seen would be the death of me should I
allow myself to be caught. I was a loose end, a huge risk to
everything they were doing - whatever insane thing that
might be.

I pulled one of the candles out of my pocket, struck a
match on the bare stone wall and lit it up. Almost
immediately, all the vague impressions I had sprang vividly
to life, even in the poor light of the flame. Not much to
speak of - a few empty crates here, some discarded
newspapers there and a couple of grimy beer bottles in one
corner of that vault. I saw an archway leading ahead and
briskly walked through it. I still had no clear plan but at
least if I was constantly moving forward that way I was
putting more distance between myself and whoever might
come after me. I moved through the next empty chamber
towards what appeared to be the exit. Walking slowly now
so as not to put the flame out, I was aware the smell of
damp stone was growing stronger - but still there were no
doors or windows anywhere, no hint of escape I could see.
I had to think of something, I knew my life now depended
solely on getting out of that place.

Debris and dust crunched underfoot as I moved
through the labyrinth as carefully as I could. The next
chamber was much the same - and the next. I realised that
in the haste of escape, those moments where I'd first run

blindly through the corridors and chambers had cost me my precious sense of direction. To make things worse, I could also tell from the constant muffled level of the thumping disco that I still seemed to be far too close to the main club area - I'd probably been walking round in wide circles in the dark.

Eventually I stopped in a room where I could see some light ahead. I stepped through the connecting archway and saw distinct shafts of blending coloured light shining across the room horizontally. I saw there was a bright, pulsating rectangular grid projecting on to the wall on my right. It took me a few seconds to work out what I was looking at. I blew out the candle.

I traced the beams of light back to their source, a metal grate set in the wall around eye level to my left. This seemed to be an air vent of sorts, presumably into the Club, through which the streams of light and sound were escaping. My breathing still laboured, I edged around the wall to the side of the grate and peered through.

The vent was big enough to see past what looked like a few layers of brick and then into the main part of the Club beyond. From what I could see in the coloured lights it looked as if this was one of the alcoved recesses surrounding the dance floor. I flexed up on my toes and found that if I looked down I could see a partially obscured table littered with wine glasses and cigarette packets. There were shapes around the table of at least three diners. The music lulled and the sound of chatting and conversation became more audible for a brief moment. Then the music resumed - the voices fell away as the trancelike intro began to an Underworld anthem, a track that meant so much to me back in the day. Strangely, it made my heart lift - it was exhilarating. Looking through this window into the Club it was as if I could feel the music even more intensely, as if my connection to everything in here - the people, the lights, the music - was hardwired. All I could do was listen as the intro played out and wait until that tribal bass drum began. When it did, it was as if every beat pulsed through me, as if each kick was some short burst of high energy reaching out into me from the next room - the sensation was overwhelming.

I flapped back around to rest against the wall and straight away I felt my head spin and stomach spasm. All at once the grim scene in the kitchen, the horrors from the past and the realisation that I'd lost a friend to these butchers combined with thoughts of what (or who) was now inside my stomach from earlier. The message got through hard to my gag reflex - my guts convulsed and I finally threw up.

I buckled to my knees bending over close to the ground to try and stop the noise from carrying. The pain in my stomach racked my whole body and it felt as if every nerve was straining with the effort.

Then, after a few brief seconds, it was over. Thankfully, in the darkness at ground level I couldn't see the detail in whatever I'd puked. I wiped the tears from my eyes and pulled myself up to the vent again, doing my best to avoid standing in my own sludge. I tried to get a better look at who was sitting beyond. The metal grate didn't afford a clear view - I could make out the top of a thin and intense looking balding man's head, the side view of a smaller, younger man with thick dark hair dressed in casual clothes and the occasional glimpse of a pretty girl with shoulder length dark hair in a black polo neck smoking a cigarette. The grate seemed to be positioned partly above their heads so their conversation could be separated - with some effort - from the throb of the music. I strained to listen and found I could pick out bits and pieces of their chat. They seemed to be gossiping about the other people in the Club.

"Well, I think it's a pretty poor show, myself," said the balding man, "Word is there just wasn't enough to go around until the girls made that catch earlier. I say he's just not up to it. It's ironic really, nothing ever changes – just another incompetent French Captain."

"Oh, come on, Pierre's done alright in the past, and you've got to admit it's turned out well enough!" said the man in casuals.

"Yeah, but if it hadn't been for the girls it all would have been pretty pathetic, all that bloody distance for nothing," Balding complained, "I reckon he's just winging it - always thought as much."

"Fuck's sake, there's no pleasing some folk is there?" said Casuals, "I'm sure he would have had something else up his sleeve - he's a resourceful old bastard is our Pierre."

"But it's just not *traditional*, is it? I mean, what if there was going to be an Initiation or Ascension tonight? We'd at least need a..."

Suddenly there was a whoop and cheer from the main part of the Club way beyond my line of vision - all three guests turned around to look then all smiled and clapped simultaneously.

"YEEEEESSSS!" cheered the man in casuals. After a few seconds the conversation resumed. This time it was the girl who led on in a husky voice, "Hey, what does it matter anyway? As long as they check out okay, one Longpig tastes pretty much the same as the next, doesn't it?"

Balding took umbrage at this, "No, no, no, NO!" he whined, "That's just missing the whole point!" I saw the skin on top of his head shake slowly in despair, "You'll understand once you've been part of this as long as us - it's not only about *tasting* the meat - it's what you can *know* through it - the *assimilation*. These ceremonies should be treated with *reverence* - we're dealing with the frontiers of human experience here - the *absorption* of forbidden knowledge, the blending of minds as well as the greatest taboo." The balding man looked as if he knew he was wasting his breath, "You know yourself the difference it makes – all the more sharper senses and instincts? That feeling of *knowing* through another? I mean what's the point of it all if not to advance the sensations and mind?"

"Oh yeah…" Husky Girl smiled mischievously and nonchalantly blew cigarette fumes into the air. She looked as if she didn't give a shit about the semantics or the drama.

"Aye, right," said Casuals and looked away, his attention now appeared drawn elsewhere.

Then it hit me - that word I'd heard Teagan whisper to Vincent back when we first stepped into the Club: *'Cochon longue'*. French for pig and French for long. Pigs long. Long pigs. Longpigs. And… jeez, I knew this. There was a 90's band called The Longpigs - and I knew where the name came from - it was a piece of useless trivia that stuck with me, as these things do if they're morbid enough. Longpigs was the slang term cannibals used for their prospective human food.

Shit. We were the Longpigs - we had been all along. It was unreal. I wondered if things might have been different if I'd made the connection earlier - but then I would probably never believe that such a thing was possible in this bar - in this city - on this night.

"Anyway," said Husky Girl, "If it wasn't for that incompetent French Captain back in the day, the Olds would never have been on the raft, never ran out of food and never been driven to taste the others - none of us would be here if it wasn't for him,"

Balding said nothing, he was having none of it. Husky Girl finally raised her hands in surrender and shook her head, she had lost interest. There was a brief pause as they all took sips from their glasses.

"So, I see they've wheeled in the display table - what do you think the final floorshow might be?" asked the girl. Balding shook his head despondently. He appeared to have taken a huff.

"Honestly, I've no idea," said Casuals. "But hey, when they fill that table it'll be great!"

Balding shook his head, "It'll probably be some pathetic last-minute drama, knowing Pierre. I'll tell you, the next time it comes around to meeting in *this* town, someone else better be doing the organis..."

Different sounds suddenly interrupted the conversation - but these were coming from behind me rather than through the vent. There were footsteps approaching on the stone floor beyond the doorway to this chamber and I judged probably the one before that too - I had a two room head start. I moved quietly away through the archway opposite, even deeper into the dusty bowels of the building. It now made me nauseous that all my senses seemed so receptive - 'all the more sharper' - it really was just like the balding guy had said.

I paused past the archway just to make sure. Yes, there was no mistaking - those were definitely approaching footsteps and there were more than just one set...

13. BARRED

I moved off again picking up the pace. I passed through at least five or six further chambers but frustratingly I never seemed to be much farther away from the pounding rhythm of the disco that seemed to constantly seep through the walls to my left. I probably still hadn't put much distance between me and the central part of the Club.

Then suddenly, unexpectedly, I had a break. I came to a room which had a choice of three exits and took a right turn, away from the source of the music - this led me into a larger, colder chamber. There didn't seem to be any arched exits from this room but at the far side I could see a flight of steps with iron railings maybe four or five feet high, which led upwards to a black recess in the wall. The movement of feet was still behind me - whoever was coming this way didn't seem to be in a hurry but they were getting closer. I decided to light another candle.

I struck up a match, lit a candle and again the whole room seemed to illuminate so I could see the features in detail - this was a small stairway that led up to a barred double fire door with a large retaining bar across it - which presumably led to the outside. Hadn't Gerry remembered this Bar having a door down the main street last time he was here? Jesus, this could be it!

I dropped the candle and saw the outlines fade slightly. Two or three bounds took me up the steps. There were two lever type handles on the doors - I lifted each one in turn but they were already both hanging loose and disengaged, obviously long broken. I felt my way around the edges and reasoned that it was held closed solely by that one metal bar slid through the brackets on the doors and walls. There were no padlocks or bolts holding it in place so it seemed as if all I needed to do to open them was to somehow slide that bar out of position. I placed my ear up against the door and found I could hear noises from outside - the swish of car tyres on wet road and the voices of the last of the clubbers making their way home.

I heaved at the door to see how strong it was and winced as a metallic rattle filled the room and the corridors behind. I realised straight away I'd given my pursuers a beacon to follow in the dark. Almost frantic now, I looked up and realised there were sliding bolts at the tops of the doors anchoring each into the frame. I pulled at both in turn and to my relief they easily turned and fell down into their sheaths. Again I hauled at the doors - this time they gave partially outwards having now been released from two of their fixings - but there was still no sign of any give from that metal bar which remained stubbornly rigid across the middle.

I grabbed on the bar and pulled hard as the sound of the footsteps moved one room closer, now crunching in the stone dust just beyond the doorway to this room.

The bar didn't move - I felt a sharp pain as my fingertips shredded against the rusting metal and the warm wet of blood mingling between my fingers.

"Fucking *fuck*!" I heard my own voice hiss in the cold as I spat the words out through the pain. I pulled again long and hard, gritting my teeth and putting my whole body into the effort. But this time the bar moved - it slid along a matter of two or three inches.

In the next room the footsteps slowed - they were joined by further footsteps, more bodies congregating. I became aware of the excited murmur of voices in the gathering crowd.

I pulled again, this time my hands slipped along the bar as it gave a little more. I heard a metallic snap as it fell free of the first metal fixing in the wall.

The excited murmur grew to occasional discernible words:

"...can hear him through here, just at the old entrance..."

"...seems a tough one – the taste suggests an interesting past..."

"...but must have known he would never escape..."

"...who the hell does he think he is anyway?"

"...bloody arse..."

Now the palms of my hands were beginning to lacerate as I clawed and grappled at the corroded metal, but it was paying off; the bar moved another few inches, almost freeing up one complete half of the door. For some reason I found the smell and taste of my own blood overpowering...

"Aha! There he is!" They were now in the room behind me.

A final push - I threw everything I had into it. The bar moved one last time then stalled with a jerk - but one complete half of the door was now completely clear. Again, I pushed at it hard - I needed to get this open, even if it was just wide enough to let me squeeze outside...

But my heart sank when the door held fast after the first couple of inches. The doors opened out just enough to let some streetlight shine in through the gap, making it easy to see there was still a solid hasp and padlock holding it fast on the outside. In my own frustration, I screamed out of the narrow opening into the empty street for someone to come, someone to help, someone to get the police - but all I heard by way of reply was the echo of desperation as my voice reflected off the walls opposite. The traffic I'd heard earlier must have passed, the homebound clubbers gone on their way.

A wash of despair consumed me and I felt everything drain - the anger, the fight, the will to survive. Everything I'd known, everything that had kept me alive in the worst of times and places in the past had deserted me in this darkened cellar, in my own home town, in the face of what I'd seen these people do to others purely for their own self-indulgence.

I turned to face my pursuers and saw their shapes still gradually fill the room. I could see some of their faces, now amber lit by the streetlight shining through the gap in the doors behind me. It was as if they were all standing back in some sort of perverse anticipation, like voyeurs enjoying this final surge of despair as I finally realised they were right: there *was* no escaping this Club. I heard a woman giggle lightly amongst the crowd. I turned around to the doors again and threw my fingers between them in a final effort to prise them open while at the same time screaming as hard as I could - to no one and nothing beyond.

I was still screaming when I felt the pressure of long, muscular arms close around my neck and torso from behind. As I struggled best I could with the last of my energy, some sort of cloth was clamped over my mouth and I found myself overcome by the sickly-sweet tang of chemicals and antiseptic. Almost immediately, my head began to lighten and spin.

Resigned though I was, I still dug deep and struggled - I fought the best I could, even though I knew it was hopeless. After everything I'd survived in the past there was no way I wanted to go out like this – but nothing seemed enough to shift those iron grips or lift the lightness in my head that now seemed to be draining my sight. I felt my legs fail and my consciousness slip away to the sound of deep throated chuckling and the scraping noise my boots made in the dust as I was dragged away backwards.

14. FLOORSHOW

I seemed to come around in stages. At first I was comfortable and euphoric, I could easily have been in my own bed at home realising this was all just some sick fever dream, but then my body began to wise up. My head hurt, my chest felt heavy and numb, my closed eyes were restless and painful, already hinting at the agony waiting when I fully came to. Then as the fog around my memory began to lift, I realised the source of pain in my head was a bright light shining directly above my face through closed eyelids. Piece by piece, my recollections returned and the vivid fear, horror and grief which had driven me just before passing out re-emerged, flooding through me as sheer panic. I tried struggling dopily but felt little response from any part of my body. I became aware of voices chattering amongst themselves all around. Again, I found I could make out snippets of what was being said…

"...seems to be coming out of it..." said the familiar voice of a girl I somehow knew.

"…will be very interesting what we'll learn from this one…"

"…not long now…"

"...and it's always much more fun when..."

But again, everything began to fade. It seemed the more I faded away, the less pain, panic and fear I felt - it was hard to resist, I didn't fight it. The voices began to dissolve as I drifted comfortably away to a distant but familiar black place.

A distant black place from a previous life. I found myself back in the memory that seemed impossible for Gerry or me to bury no matter how hard we tried. Once again, I was standing in the moonlight of the Afghan plains. At first it was like a fleeting, sleepy memory that might just pass, but something made me want to hold it there on my way towards losing all consciousness and getting out for good. In my anaesthetised, traumatised mind I was back again that night on the cold sand of the Dasht-e Margo desert, a distance of over two years and three and a half thousand miles, standing back in that rocky hollow. We knew there was a lot at stake, the local organised crime Chief's wife had wanted to defect - she was little more than a prisoner herself and probably saw the same for her girls if they even lived long enough to grow up. Her proposition had been to tell us all she knew about her husband's operations, which would likely save a lot of lives - in exchange for the guaranteed safety of her and her daughters. And it had all gone well, even though she told us from the off she thought her husband was on to her. So far it had all gone to plan. We had already sneaked the family out of the compound, the guards were all either sleeping or drunk, so no firefight.

We had led them up the rocky hillsides from the camp towards the extraction zone - then as we all regrouped and did a headcount we realised we had one too many, another girl who must have seen us during the climb and tagged along. We knew the hills were rife with fanatical spies and spotters for the Chief, entire families made crazy with devotion by keeping them in food, clothes and money and making promises straight from God. Young girl or not, everyone there knew how much risk this uninvited guest brought with her, especially if he already suspected they might betray him.

Gerry raised his weapon but none of us knew which girl was the imposter as we were all using night sights and the dark Burqas all looked too similar in the low light lenses. The mother began shouting in Dari and quickly the girls began to separate, as if they sensed each other, leaving one standing apart from the group. We had seconds to assess and decide what to do - but in the very first of those, she raised one hand high, showing us a hand grenade which we all saw had lost its pin. Then the noise began all around, the girls screaming for their lives when they realised this passenger, an infiltrator no older than the rest of the kids there, was prepared to die in return for taking their lives - and ours - for whatever she'd been promised in the next world by the Chief.

There was no way to isolate her as we were in a natural shelter and there was nowhere to go. The girls screamed more, they knew they were going to die. The surrounding rocks magnified the cries to a deafening level. I saw Gerry drop his gun, trying to manoeuvre himself, turning so as to shield them with whatever his body armour could offer. Then, just before the sudden hot flash that one way or another, ended the moment for all of us - the time in my head seemed to slow, as if reminding me painfully of everything we lost in the hollow that night. Gerry and I were wounded, shrapnelled and cut in every way possible but we were lucky - the body armour took most of it and we lived through it, which was more than anyone else did.

I knew at the time it was a memory - but it felt real. There was ringing in my ears, panic in my chest and my body felt like it was full of hot needles - all the grief and anger surged back. I could hear them all screaming again, no easing from the medication, no perspective silencing them, no dulling with the passage of time. They were real and standing beside me as I lay drifting on that table in the Club. I steeled myself and took a sharp breath in - I still knew where I was really - I knew I had to fight the comfort of simply slipping away. I realised how much breathing hurt, it felt like hammers pounding me hard about the chest.

Then slowly, the bright light came back. Gentle chatter in the room began to return to underpin the howling in my ears. I suddenly found I was aware of being able to move my own arms and legs in their bindings. I was coming back into my body with the screams now at the front of my mind dragging me back from that all too convenient, pointless way out. The screams had brought me back.

I knew it would hurt like Hell but I tried to make myself rigid. I breathed in deeply and sent that breath to every part of my body. Then, as if trawling up my final reserves of energy, I fought the last of the blackness inside and gritted my teeth against that eager black cloud I'd almost surrendered to. I heard myself moan as I flexed my arms and legs in an effort to restart my body.

"Ah, here he comes!" I heard a male voice announce in a sickly, cheerful tone.

"Oh, superb!" said a familiar girl's voice. Keisha.

I then knew I'd returned, or at least - to a certain extent. Again, I tried to struggle but this time I felt firm resistance around my arms and legs. I heard a gentle round of applause as I painfully opened my eyes and looked into the light above me - which was a square, overhanging box light that looked as if it may have served over a snooker or pool table in a previous life. I lifted my head slightly and realised my predicament in an instant. I had been laid on my back on some sort of freestanding table, tied tightly around my arms and legs in an arrangement that felt like binds connected beneath me. I was the floorshow.

As the polite applause continued I realised my body felt cold, there was cool air drafting over my skin. At that point the light above my face was switched off and my surroundings fell better into focus. I heaved my head up as far as I could and as quickly as the glare from the light dissolved, I began to see shapes and colours fall into place around the room. I saw I was undressed, the remains of my clothes lying in pieces on the table by my side, as if they had been cut off with surgical care in situ, like some kind of casualty in a rushed emergency procedure.

I moved my head from side to side and saw I was surrounded in this helpless state by almost everyone I remembered seeing in the Club since I first walked in. They were all smiling - they all seemed to be in some kind of happy state of anticipation.

Then the applause slowly petered out and stopped - but to my horror, the crowd all seemed to take a step in towards me, closer, eagerly watching, as if anticipating some other impending event. As the fear rose back in me I tried to scream, but the sound I made never amounted to anything more than a choking gargle near the bottom of my throat.

I was aware of two forms approaching me from either side - familiar somehow - Gerry's anaesthetists, the men he'd gone off with Teagan to look for just before they both disappeared. And then two unexpected sharp pains: one in my right arm, the other in the left side of my neck.

"Relax old boy, these will help you enjoy *your* part of the fun just that *little bit more...*"

I felt the pressure increase beneath the pains and realised I was probably being given some sort of surgical injections. I closed my eyes and tried to struggle in an effort to keep moving. Strangely, I felt a surge of adrenaline, as if my body were trying to fight the drugs being forced into me.

Then more fragments of detached discussions,

"...wonderfully clever you know, it isolates muscle movement but doesn't disrupt the sense of touch..."

"...dissolves in the stomach juices so it won't affect anyone's digestion – so there should be no nasty cases of heartburn afterwar ..."

"...it's just so clever, what modern medicine can do..."

As my body became heavy everything around me became louder, brighter, more intense – it was as if I'd lost all movement, but my other senses were heightening to compensate, maybe even more so if what I heard the Bald man say was true. Then, just as I reached a point where the colours and sounds were becoming overwhelming, there was a warm, fleshy sensation all over my body - a soft, perfumed smoothness that brushed lightly over my face just before I heard Keisha's voice in my ear.

"Don't worry, our two friends here know exactly just how much sedative you'll need, so you can still have fun too. We're going to enjoy you so much my darling..." I shuddered as I felt the warm wet of her mouth trailing slowly from my ear down to my chest. Then a voice at the other side of my head. Teagan.

"Relax, my baby - it's all becoming so much clearer - I'm beginning to see it all now - and it's all so sad. I can tell, you know, just like I could taste the music in your past, it seems some things really are in the blood..."

I felt the warmth of her mouth on the other side of my head as it began to trace down to where Keisha was lingering around my stomach. I felt perverse - disgusted with myself for feeling the pleasure they were giving me and for wanting it to go on forever...

I was stalled. In my mind it even felt as if the screams of the desert girls were now petering out, as if they'd spent all their energy coming back from my past - and having done that, I'd let them down by not being able to fight hard enough. It was understandable, why would distant ghosts or anyone else bother themselves any further? What was the point? What did I really matter? It was all over, all I could do was wait for the darkness to fall that one last time.

Teagan must have anticipated my questions and slowly kissed her way back to around my right ear.

"But you know *how much you matter — and you know why - you've seen what ties us all together..."*

I tried to speak, to plead, but could only manage a frustrating gasp in my throat.

"It's the secret only the few can know. It has pleasures and tastes and benefits you're only beginning to feel!" I felt her hand stroke down the length of my exposed torso and writhed as I felt another sharp pressure, Keisha biting into the area around my groin.

I wished I could ask her what she meant, but the drugs had taken such a hold of me that I now couldn't make any sound at all.

"Sshhh, don't worry my darling, you don't have to speak. It's the flesh and the blood that gives the knowledge - the mind, the memory, the spirit - the flesh is just a vessel for them to flow through. Most believe sex is the closest two people can be - but there's so much more. To truly taste someone, to have them dissolve in you, for two to literally become one, to feel the thoughts and sights, the sounds and desires of another life mingle with your own. Here, just look..." Teagan gently slipped her hand behind my head and tilted it up so I could see down the length of my own body,

"How do you think I can hear what you're thinking? How do you think my voice is here among all your other thoughts?"

I looked down and was met by the sight of Keisha, unclothed and lying spread across my numb legs, her face bloodied with the same tribal smear I'd seen across Teagan's eyes earlier. Her head was level with my stomach, traces of thick, dark blood stained her mouth and upper body. In her left hand she held a glinting surgical scalpel and, in her right, a long, bloody strip of my own freshly cut flesh. She looked ecstatic as she flipped her head back and devoured the flesh raw. As Teagan lifted my head higher I could see a large section of my chest and stomach had already been carefully carved away - a tangle of transparent tubes fed directly into the open wounds around my torso from a collection of drips and bags which hung suspended on metal stands by the table. My stomach - almost comically - was lined at both sides with salad, sauces and garnishes from the table spread earlier in the night.

Teagan then cradled my head so I could face her again and in my utter numbness I saw her smile, genuinely - wide and loving. As she bared her teeth, I saw a small sliver of meat drop from the side of her mouth.

"Just think, lover," she whispered, *"Soon I'll know all you've ever been or dreamed of..."*

I tried to snap my head back in the horror of it all but nothing was working, nothing was listening. I was aware of Teagan gently laying my head back down on the table which now felt soft and insubstantial around my head.

Now my own mind began to scream - but my body couldn't follow. I felt the soft sensation of Teagan's skin retreat down the length of my body to continue the work she had already begun.

But as I lay dissolving into my last moments, I became aware of something else in the room. Suddenly there were voices that seemed out of place. Then my mind caught a final fragment of puzzled words just before it shut down completely,

"How the Hell did they get in here...?"

15. DEAD?

Those last few seconds were a confusing blur as it was difficult to separate the sounds in the room from the streams of alien words that were now forming in my own mind. I felt crashing noises surround me and the soft, warm pressure suddenly lift from my body - then I sensed a sudden rush of fear and panic jump like static between everyone in the room. I remember a sensation of urgency then a movement of air and the draining of peripheral colour as my audience hastily departed. I became aware of more voices in the room and some stunted screams, orders being given and feet moving heavily, quickly and efficiently. Then I was surrounded by new voices, a different audience and the overwhelming sensation of horror and disbelief all around.

I was aware of strangers shouting in my ear, asking me somewhat stupidly if I was okay and if I was in any pain. I tried to move something, give some sort of response – but there was nothing left in me, it was as if I was locked inside myself. Then there was the sensation of rising upwards, of all sensation around my body being released. I remember passing into an acidic smelling, dreamless void as the new voices in both the room and my head became all the more distant.

I guess it was then I finally did escape Club Medusa.

*

So how can I be here telling you this? Am I dead? Is this one of those stories where the narrator turns out to be a ghost? Or, did I finally wake up in bed to find it was all just some kind of night terror? I wish.

No to all of the above. The truth is, I'm not exactly sure myself what happened next. After the Club, my next memory was a bright room and hearing distorted voices of what I imagined were either doctors, police or priests giving me snippets of unwelcome information, as if probing for some sort of response. Again, all their conversations sounded patchy:

"...after we were told someone was trapped in the old nightclub..."

"...you sounded like the men we had been looking for..."

"...we had never seen anything like that up close..."

"...they all vanished like rats down drains..."

"...it was almost as if they could see in the dark..."

"...they seemed to anticipate everything we did..."

"...you were lucky - just on the brink..."

"...we've never known anyone to survive after they..."

"...seemingly..."

So, I guess what I'm telling you is that right now - I'm not dead. I must have mattered enough for someone to get me out of there before I bled out. I'm guessing I'm in some sort of recovery - but I don't know where or how I got here - no one has explained that one yet. I suppose I might have been heard after all when I screamed out of those fire doors? Maybe some of those drunken clubbers heard the screams and broke in, which I suppose could be possible, especially with everyone inside distracted by the floorshow. I expect the authorities or whoever wouldn't have been too far behind - but those footsteps I'd heard sounded purposeful, tactical - almost military - but I don't get the impression I'm in any military place now, everyone here seems too measured, too presentable.

From what I think I've heard amongst the drifting snippets, it also sounds as if none of the diners were caught that night, though I suppose that isn't a huge surprise, considering the labyrinth I passed through trying to escape the Club. If even one of them knew the layout, they could have led the rest out elsewhere on the block before anyone realised what was happening – the same tactic Gerry and I used when we escaped the mob from Lady's.

Anyway, whoever found me would probably be too numb from the sights of the buffet to want to chase those particular culprits down into the darkness. Probably for the best, I don't want anyone else's blame for how that could have ended. It was bad enough that after everything Gerry and I had learned the hard way, we were still only too happy to fall into that expertly timed honey trap purely because it suited us. In a way I suppose it serves us right for believing any of their bullshit. What did we matter to anyone in that Club anyway? Who cared about us really? The truth is we were nothing to them other than fodder. If any of them did care, it was only as much as you might care yourself for the quality of your own next meal or evening's entertainment.

But that's all history now. To be honest I'm not much good at getting to grips with what's happening outside my head these days - and even then, I'm not sure I really want to anyway. Even if they do save the parts of me I occasionally hear them talking about, even if they do get me back to 'mostly functioning' again, I doubt I would ever have a mind quiet enough to enjoy any sort of life again.

You see, since I've come in here I've had two regular visitors.

Not to my room - not visitors in that sense - visits to my mind. They still talk to me. They know what I'm thinking of. They seem to know everything I've ever been or dreamed of.

"And tonight lover, we're going to do it all again. This time - Berlin!"

Oh God, they're here again.

"Pierre's found the most wonderful place this time around!"

"Keisha?"

"Teagan?"

"Is that you..?"

Club Medusa will re-open soon...

16. BASED ON TRUE STORIES: A BRIEF HISTORY OF CLUB MEDUSA

This story has been with me in one form or another for more years than I'd like to admit. So, with the Club and me having a bit of a long-term relationship, I thought it might be worth putting a few words down about the true (and maybe not so true) stories and inspiration that brought it all to life.

Club Medusa originally began life as part of a much bigger project I began in the late 90s. It was a standalone tale (originally called Club Batak) written alongside a number of others, all intended to be part of one big book with a connecting story arc through it. I wanted this big book to be like one of those old Amicus horror movies, with Peter Cushing in charge, a group of seemingly random people telling their own stories in some way - then at the end, a punchline, usually something like, "What? We're all actually dead already? *Nooooo….!*"

Okay, well my punchline was way weirder than that, but you get the idea. It was all good fun and a lot of work at the time – but to be honest, it all became a bit convoluted as I ended up having to alter and ditch ideas to make everything fall in line with the overall plan. Long story short, I completed the manuscript - but it was rejected by every publisher who bothered to look at it. I did get some encouraging comments about my writing at the time from a couple of people in the business but it wasn't long before I had a bad experience with an agent - and then it all stalled. This created a void which was quickly filled by the day job and then children. Next thing I knew, everything I'd written was on a shelf gathering dust.

Fast forward to a serious return to writing last year which began with a review of everything I'd written previously to see if anything might still fly. So, as I re-read that original huge manuscript, besides cringing in some places, I did find that both Club Med and another story, Joey by David, still jumped out as being pieces I was very pleased with. It didn't seem right to just forget about them and plough into something new. And so, with a bit of editing, tightening up some vagueness and bringing everything up to date (there were no mobile phones in the original – now the damn things rule our lives!), the story developed into the version you've (hopefully) just read.

As to where the specific idea came from, that's all a bit trickier to explain. I seem to remember three different sources, all things that were in my head at that time. The first was a bizarre magazine article I'd read back then about 'Cannibal Rats.' This piece described some 'scientific' experiment where lab rats were taught how to navigate a maze – were then killed – and then had their brains fed to a bunch of new rats who, bizarrely, were able to navigate the same maze, seemingly without being shown the way. Oooh, ingested intelligence through eating educated brains? Yes, it does sound like nonsense - and I can't find any source or trace of the article online despite the amount of tosh on Google – but the idea stuck with me as it was just so grotesque and weird.

The second piece of wholesome inspiration was probably a number of escapades I had around that same certain time in my life when I still spent many a night partying in town with friends and colleagues. Although I'm no angel, I've never really been a huge drinker myself, so I often found I would end up being the voice of comparative sanity at the end of the night trying to talk peers with alcohol induced high confidence issues out of blagging their way into Clubs and making arses of themselves. I didn't always succeed. In fact, I don't think I *ever* succeeded, but some of the hilarious and disastrous consequences did serve as part inspiration for this cautionary tale. Though I don't remember any of us being eaten back then. Well, not many of us.

The third thing is way more dull and conventional, it almost sounds like the sort of thing a proper author would say, but it was my lifelong interest in Edinburgh's history, especially the Old Town. When I was about eight or nine years old, my parents gave me a short book called The Ghosts, Witches and Worthies of the Royal Mile. I loved that book and all the stories in it: Mary Kings Close, Deacon Brodie, Major Weir and his evil walking stick, Half-hanged Maggie Dickson – all the scary greatest hits were there and most happened in places I could go and look at if I pestered my parents hard enough. Must admit, I've never really grown out of that – I still love strange local stories and visiting the places to soak up the vibes. Maybe that's a pastime that should have a proper name?

Anyway, that was one of the main reasons I wanted all the action to happen in and around the Cowgate. That part of town really is a hub for nightlife just like in the story, but at the same time, the nightclubs and neon bars are still surrounded by hundreds of years of history and also not far from the scenes of many of my favourite grisly tales. I wanted the Old Town to play a part in shaping events and maybe also remind readers how much of a past there is down there when they're staggering back from the bars at 3am. And if I could scare the crap out of some people along the way, that would be nice too. I hope I succeeded in at least some of it.

It's maybe also worth mentioning, especially to readers unfamiliar with Edinburgh, that all the geography and place names mentioned are real. Most of the clubs were real too at some point – but most are just shout outs to great places from times gone by. Shady Lady's, for example, the backstreet Club where Gerry and Paul end up brawling with the door staff, really was the name of the Club there in the late 80s. You would find Lady's (often with me and some of my chums in it) at the basement level of the Club complex in Victoria Street which over the years has been known as Nicky Tams, The Mission and Espionage – and undoubtedly a few more before those. Shady's was at the very bottom part of the building and could be accessed directly off the Cowgate – almost a back door. And it's also true that, although I have fond memories of the place, it could be a bit ropey at times.

Sadly, the whole complex seems to have closed down for good over the last year or so – the end of another era I suppose.

Then there's Club Medusa itself and all who sail in her. Okay, I made most of that up – but there are many bars and clubs in the Old Town you could easily walk into and believe you'd just stepped into the same venue in the book. Many of the nightspots in that part of town really are old tenement cellar labyrinths with bare brick walls and bathrooms you might never find your way back from in one piece.

It's also true that there really is a large painting in the Louvre called Raft of the Medusa. Painted by Theodore Gericault in 1818-19, it's impressive, dark and terrifying, especially if you know the history. So, although they were being understandably vague, Teagan and Keisha were pretty much spot on. Also, the story really was a big deal in its day and the French Captain really did get the blame along with the French King at the time for allowing the Captains appointment. I didn't want the characters to give a history lesson in the story, but to put the Medusa tragedy in perspective, over the 13 days drifting at sea, the 147 survivors on the raft from the shipwreck were reduced to only 15 – and those who remained really did have nowhere else to turn but the only remaining food source. That's what I'd call real horror.

Obviously my Medusans all scattered at the end of the story, but if you ever feel the urge to visit the street where the Club was the night our heroes bagged an invite, the location is Merchant Street, west of Dyer's Close, just beyond the low archway supporting George IV Bridge.

Coincidentally, it's almost directly underneath The Elephant House Coffee Shop, where JK Rowling allegedly wrote some of the first Harry Potter book – which by my reckoning would have been written around the same time I was writing the very first sketchy draft of Club Med. How's that for a tale of contrasting successes...?

Finally, back in the day when I originally wrote the first drafts of this tale, there was nothing beyond or below the iron railings where Teagan and Keisha are first seen other than steep, stone steps and a few dark and anonymous doorways. Believe it or not, there are now a couple of fairly upmarket restaurants down there. I wonder what their specialty is? Do you think they do buffets?

In any case, I'll have a Chardonnay…

Martin White
East Lothian (in Lockdown), April 2020

ABOUT THE AUTHOR

Martin White has had an unusual career path - Paper Delivery Boy, Restaurant Cleaner and Coleslaw Maker, Print Finisher, Musician, Police Officer, Photographer, Author - some of those things are not like the others...

Originally from the Scottish fishing town of Musselburgh, he's spent most of his life living between there, Edinburgh and now a quaint village in East Lothian where he's found a lot more lurking under the picture postcard surface than most people would like to believe. He's pretty sure there's probably a book in there somewhere.

With a lifelong interest in dark and macabre writing and anything else in life that's odd, surreal or just plain strange, he sets out to tell stories where unlikely and often terrifying things happen to normal people living their lives in ordinary places.

When he's not writing scary stories, he can usually be found playing guitar somewhere.

For further information and updates:

Blog
www.martinwhiteauthor.com

Twitter: @Martinwhite14

Facebook
www.facebook.com/Martin-White-Author-Page/

Instagram
www.instagram.com/martinwhiteauthor/

Music
martinwhiteguitar.bandcamp.com
theyounggorgiesurfteam.bandcamp.com

Also available on Amazon Kindle by Martin White:

Joey by David

Most children have imaginary friends at one time or another - people, cartoon characters, animals, even favourite toys come to life, it's all normal behaviour.

But when do these friends stop being imaginary? Is it when they start doing magic tricks in the real world? When they start showing their child how to control the world around them? When they begin to terrify parents for fun? What about when they decide they just don't like your real friends?

Surely that's more than just imaginary?

David's imaginary friend Joey has been around since before he can remember. He might look weird and move strangely - but only David can see him and only David can hear him.

This puts David in a place between the real world and somewhere else entirely.

Somewhere that's truly terrifying…

Printed in Great Britain
by Amazon

58708925R00073